W9-BWS-008

DETROIT PUBLIC LIBRARY
3 5674 00752539 8

THE CHAPLAINS RAID

RIC HARDMAN

The Chaplains Raid

"Sweet is war to him who knows it not."

—PINDAR

Coward-McCann, Inc. New York

Library of Congress Catalog Card Number: *65-13272*

MANUFACTURED IN THE UNITED STATES OF AMERICA

To Christopher and Regan
who are bound to be somebody's
Charlie and Ella.

SERGEANT HERZOG came into the tent wiping rain from his face. "Gooks and Wogs," he grumbled, "Gooks and Wogs!" He left a trail of mud, dropped his carbine and helmet on the cot and stripped out of his dungaree blouse baring a vast, dark-haired chest. "Gooks and Wogs," he said again as he dried himself on a fungus-green towel. "Gooks and goddamned Wogs!"

The rain beat down on the tent, cooling the sultry air. The old-style brass dog tags on the chain around Herzog's neck chinked like Siamese finger cymbals as he scrubbed himself with the towel. He dug another blouse out of his foot locker and put it on, breathing deeply, snorting and shaking his head like he had a mosquito in his ear.

I turned the soggy page of the book I was reading, *Moral Man and Immoral Society*, by Reinhold Niebuhr.

"I said 'Gooks and Wogs!' " Herzog bawled.

"I know."

"Danbom, today I'm going to kill you."

I closed my book and dropped it into a box with the others beside my cot. "How was the hunt?" I asked.

Herzog sat down on his cot and began to clean his carbine. "A freaking disaster," he said. "A great big freaking disaster!"

"Sorry to hear it," I said.

"Sorry hell! You don't give a damn, never did, never will. You should have been up there today. Big John Fischer had to go down after that Gook in the rice paddies; nothing would do him but to go down. I warned him the rain was coming, but Big John wanted a foot race so down we went, six copters full of troops into the mud. One copter hit a soft shoulder trying to land on one of those goddamned bullock roads, tilted over and bent the rotor blades all to hell. All to hell!"

"Anyone hurt?"

"No, but leaving that copter behind made a very expensive captive."

"So you got him."

"Sure we got him! One copter stayed up and kept knocking him over with the rotor blast until we were on the ground and sloshing through the paddies after him with Captain Fischer, mud up to his knees, running with his carbine at high port yelling that Texas lullaby of his. At sixty to one how in hell shouldn't we get him? He ran like hell, but with all us advisers and troops on his tail, he finally just gave up and stood there waiting. Looked about sixteen, weighed about ninety pounds, muddy."

"Dangerous," I said.

"Oh, sure!" Herzog grumbled. "Sure, you bet. He mighta had the measles." Herzog sighed disparagingly.

"Jesus! If I'd caught him on a trout rod I'da thrown him back, but Fischer takes him for interrogation."

I sat up on the edge of my cot, lit a cigarette and flipped it to Herzog. "Forget it," I said.

Herzog plucked the cigarette off his blanket before it scorched and took a drag. "Christ," he complained, "even the tobacco tastes green out here." He read the label on the cigarette and shook his head some more. "I don't get it," he said. "I just don't get it." He looked up, frowning. "You know what that kid said, the first words he said after he decided we weren't going to eat him?"

I shook my head.

"He looks at Captain Fischer and in English you could just about understand he says: 'Sir, is there really a Disneyland?' Fischer dang near croaked. 'Sir, is there really a Disneyland?' I thought Fischer was going to let the mud swallow him, but damned if he didn't gulp a couple of times and kind of cloud over. 'Yes, boy,' Fischer says, 'there is a Disneyland.' Well, you can kick my ass if that kid didn't grin fit to bust his jaw. He started to spiel and the interpreter says he wants to go there, says that kid would do anything to see Disneyland!"

Herzog slammed the clip back into his carbine and shot the bolt home. "Danbom!" he cried. "Danbom, what in hell kind of war is it you could win by running a guided tour to Disneyland? How in hell does a kid clear out here in the lousy jungle hear about Disneyland?"

"Communications," I said.

"Communications my tail! It's part of a goddamned Communist plot!"

Herzog stood up, flicked the cigarette into the mud beyond the tent flap and racked his carbine beside his cot. He crossed to the door sill, kicked the mud off his boots and stood there sucking air, looking at the rain. "So, you're leaving tomorrow?" he said presently. "Home and mother."

"Yeah, if you don't kill me."

"Give me a reason and I might get around to it," Herzog said spiritlessly.

"I won't go out of my way."

"You never have," he said.

Far off beyond the overlay of slate cloud the sun was shining; in another twenty minutes the rain would pass and the ground would begin to steam. Herzog sighed and returned to his cot to remove his boots. "Disneyland," he grumbled. "Danbom, have you ever seen such a screwed-up operation in your whole life? Have you ever?"

Herzog massaged his feet and the freckles bunched on his forehead as he studied his white toes. He ran his fingers between them extracting bits of lint and whatever. He was melancholy.

"Forget it, Sarge," I said.

"Yeah, yeah, easy to say."

"You're too thoughty, Sarge. It doesn't go with jungle living."

"I was all right until I bunked in with you," Herzog complained. "You're the one with all the goddamned imagination, with the reading and the line of horseshit."

"Herzog," I said calmly, "you're mistaken. You're a hundred and eighty degrees wrong about the imagination. I abjure it."

"Oh, crap!"

"No, truly, from my early youth."

"Lay off!"

"Didn't I ever tell you about Peter Pan and Tinker Bell?"

Herzog groaned. He probed his foot locker for a fresh pair of socks and pulled them on.

"When I was about ten years old at the Interdenominational Home for Boys, you know—"

"Yeah, yeah!" Herzog said.

"Yes, well, when I was about ten a church group put on this play called *Peter Pan.* Do you know it?"

"Will you knock it off!" Herzog cried.

"This will broaden your horizons, Herzog. It may explain why the kid was happy to know that there really is a Disneyland."

"Yeah? O. K. Shoot."

"Well, there's a part in the play where the boy who never wants to grow up, played by a chunky lady in tights, steps to the front of the stage while the little fairy, Tinker Bell, is dying."

"A fairy?"

"Yes, her name was Tinker Bell. They had this light rigged on stage with a pair of gauze wings, and Tinker Bell had been poisoned and she was dying. The light kept flickering up and down. Poor Tinker Bell."

"Oh, crap!"

"So there we were, forty orphans, watching Tinker Bell flicker and Peter Pan comes up front, gives a little bounce, a cheery grin, and says that the only way for us to save Tinker Bell's life is for all of us who truly believe in fairies to clap our hands. Not one kid of forty lifts a mitt. In the first place we think this Peter Pan is nuts for not wanting to grow up since our main ambition in life is to grow up and get out of Interdom as fast as possible. In the second place, we weren't enthusiastic enough about fairies to make spectacles of ourselves by clapping for one.

"Well, this poor lady, Peter Pan, was real hung. Tinker Bell was flickering up and down and bobbing around on the end of the electric cord. Peter Pan gives a hop and pats her hands together and begins to wheedle. 'Come now, children,' she wheedles, 'why, don't you know every time a little boy says he doesn't believe in fairies that a fairy somewhere falls down dead?'

"This notion pleased us some, gave us a sense of power we hadn't known we possessed, but none of us were about to clap, no sir. So it looked like the play was about to fizzle out.

"Peter Pan looked toward the flies, kind of distracted. Tinker Bell is croaking. She, Peter, I mean, starts to clap herself, but the point has gone out of the whole thing.

"Then Brother Queen, one of our teachers, a Catholic, turns to Benny Cohen, a kid about nine years old. 'Clap, Benny,' Queen hisses at the kid. 'Clap a little, clap for Tinker Bell.' So Benny, who's new to the school, claps his hands. Well, you can guess how happy Peter Pan was. You can guess. She grinned and chortled and the play went on."

"Tinker Bell came to life, right?" Herzog asked.

I nodded. "Yeah, Tinker Bell came to life, but Benny Cohen died."

Herzog frowned, then his eyes narrowed dangerously. "Died? What of?" he demanded.

"Clapping for Tinker Bell," I said.

"Now, God damn it!" Herzog cried. "God damn it, nobody dies of clapping for Tinker Bell!" He pointed at me menacingly. "Danbom, I swear you'll never get on that plane tomorrow! What did that kid die of?"

"Actually, Benny ran away. After all, one kid who professes his belief in fairies, even under coercion, can't live with thirty-nine who don't. Benny was an outcast, so he ran away."

"What did he die of?" Herzog demanded.

"He got hit by a news truck."

"That's not from clapping for Tinker Bell. The kid got run over."

"All the way you look at it, Herzog," I said. "And since that time, with one exception, I have abjured all imaginary and mythological things."

Herzog snorted, hoisted his feet up on his cot and lay back with his hands caught behind his head.

The weight of the rain increased, it came down in sheets, slashing the tent, then diminishing only to turn torrential again like a deep pulse. Herzog glanced sidelong at me. "What's that got to do with Disneyland?" he asked.

"Well, Herzog, the way I figure it is that that poor kid you captured believed in Disneyland so much that he made it come true."

"It's been true for ten years!" Herzog cried. "I was there!"

"Not for that boy. Not until today. Today he was clapping for Tinker Bell."

"Oh, mother! Will I be glad when you leave! Oh, will I rejoice! I can't wait until you fly away. I'm going to write home and tell all my people that if they ever meet a kook named Danbom, to run—just run! Then I'm going to settle down out here and be happy. Danbom, when you get out of the Corps I hope you starve." Herzog folded his arms over his ears to deaden the sound of the rain. He began to whistle tunelessly, nervously, between his clenched teeth.

"Sarge," I said presently, "I'm leaving my books for you as a gift. An idle mind is the devil's workshop, as they say."

I thought Herzog hadn't heard me and was about to repeat my bequest when he leaped to his feet, his face ruddy with outrage. "You haul those mildewed books out of here, understand, Danbom? Every goldanged, damn one of them! I've put up with enough from you! You want to get cold cocked just try me! Just try me, you dumb Greek-Indian bastard! You make me itch all over, that's what you do. Six months of itching!"

"You want to scratch, go ahead," I said.

Herzog bounded across the tent to the edge of my cot; he stood over me with his fists clenched, his face white. "I ought to smear that big nose of yours for you! I ought to bend your face!"

I pulled my feet up on the cot and clasped my hands around my cocked knees. "Sarge," I said quietly, "you're nervous."

"Ohhhh!" Herzog wailed. He threw up his hands and turned away. "Oh, mother! Oh, Christ, you make me mad!"

"Passive resistance," I said.

Herzog fell on his cot. He rolled over and stared into the peak of the tent. Gradually his breathing regulated and matched the pulse of the rain, huge slow breaths of air that filled his chest, drawing the dungaree blouse taut across his shoulders. "This is nowhere," he said, "just nowhere!"

"It's somewhere else instead," I said.

Herzog whickered, then grew quiet. There were streamers of dark rain against the lighter sky. The storm was passing away. Herzog sighed heavily and groaned.

"Danbom," he asked plaintively, "in all of recorded United States Marine Corps history has there ever been such a meatball deal? You read a lot, have you ever come across a foul-up to match this one? This ain't a war it's hide-and-go-seek, it's capture the flag and kick the can! We ain't Marines out here, we're referees; we're schoolmarms. I keep losing track of whose side I'm on!"

"That's a very serious condition, Herzog," I said sympathetically.

"These troops are all the time laughing," Herzog complained. "I get the idea they could settle this without our teaching them how to do it. Have you ever seen such a lousy foul-up?"

"I remember one very well," I said.

Herzog looked at me across the gloomy tent with the hope of a hungry dog. "What was that?" he asked.

I lit a cigarette and blew a cloud of smoke which the humidity took down to the floor like a wet rag. "Yes, yes," I said reflectively.

Herzog frowned. "What, yes, yes?" he asked.

I smiled at him through a soggy smoke ring.

"Go screw," he said. "I don't want to hear about it."

Herzog looked up into the peak of the tent once more. He crossed his arms over his chest, closed his eyes and pretended to be asleep.

I dropped my musty cigarette outside in the mud and stepped to the door.

The rain had passed. A jeep sloshed down the road toward the copter field leaving gutters of water behind the wheels. Someone laughed aloud and the sound, dampened by the moisture-laden air, was a looping necklace of laughter under the vault of clouds.

I turned to take my parka from the nail beside the door and found Herzog standing at my shoulder with a murderous expression in his eyes. He'd crossed the tent in his stocking feet, silent as a cat, and was standing there with his breath held so that I hadn't heard him approach. His right hand was rigid, flat out, ready to deliver a karate blow.

"D-Danbom, if you step through that door I'll kill you with one blow," he said with suppressed fury. "I'll split your skull."

"This too shall pass," I said.

Herzog caught the collar of my blouse and slung me down on my cot. "Tell me," he demanded.

"Tell you what?"

"About the operation that was more fouled up than this one."

"I thought you weren't interested," I said. "I thought you were asleep."

Herzog staggered to his cot, snatched his carbine from the rack and threw a shell into the chamber. "It'll be an accident," he said. "I was cleaning my carbine and it went off. An accident."

He centered the carbine on a point between my eyes which began to itch.

Herzog detected my discomfort and smiled. "You talk, Danbom," he said, "I'll just sit here and add the punctuation if I get bored."

So, under duress, and to ease poor Herzog's tormented mind, I began.

One

SUFFICE it to say that I was born in a reasonable manner and rejected shortly thereafter. My mother abandoned me and in my infancy I was shopped around to various foster homes and adoption agencies. But being a commodity lacking that surface appeal so necessary to the moving of merchandise in these eye-catching times, I was never adopted. So at the age of ten I found my home at Interdom, a charity school for unwanted boys, administered by a board of clergymen.

Here I spent seven years learning to defend my independence of mind from doctrinal persuasion and at the age of eighteen, having learned also to read, write and cipher, I joined the United States Marine Corps, went to boot camp at Parris Island and was then transferred to Camp Pendleton, California.

The chronological discrepancy which may have been detected by those with a mathematical turn of mind is due to the Marine Corps policy of not enlisting seventeen-year-olds without parental consent. Naturally I lied about my age.

I entered Pendleton aboard a six-by-six truck with two dozen replacements destined for Headquarters and Service Company, First Battalion, 16th Marines. I was even at that time something of a compulsive reader so my seabag contained, aside from the normal complement of gear, two volumes of *Evolution and Ethics* by Thomas Henry Huxley, and also a framed print of Whistler's Mother which the boys at Interdom had given me as a parting gift. She was the only mother I had.

We were driven to Las Pulgas, one of the Pendleton branch camps, a collection of permanentized Quonset huts which looked like big loaves of black rye bread set against the wheat-colored hills of California, or like beached whales with their tails lopped off. Yes, very like beached whales. The huts were sheathed in corrugated iron and accommodated a platoon apiece. They were as dreary a habitation as had ever been designed for human occupancy, clammy in the winter, hot in the summer, ugly, void of privacy and, on the inside, like being in the belly of a gutted whale—dry, but bony and cartilaginous.

Our truck stopped in the company street; we tossed our seabags down; jumped out and were greeted by Sergeant Major Eugene Strand. My seabag was at the bottom of the heap so I was the last man to fall in and Strand made me the target for his opening witticism. "Glad you decided to join us," he said.

He paced back and forth in front of us, blowing smoke from a Vesuvian cigar stuck in his craggy face. His head sat hard down on his shoulders; his waistline joined his rump with no distinguishing curvature and the seat of his trousers bagged emptily behind. Presently he planted himself, put his hands on his hips, tipped forward slightly and welcomed us.

"All right, you fats," he said, "welcome to H and S Company, First Battalion. Those of you who last the day will want to remember that my name is Sergeant Strand. The C.O. of this outfit is Colonel Haskell Pollard. He was born in the Halls of Montezuma. Any questions?"

There were no questions.

The Quonset hut to which I was assigned was just behind the Headquarters building with sixteen steel frame bunks, upper and lower, and standing metal lockers, the doors of which shrieked each time they were opened, making a sound that just about tore the nerves out by the roots.

The lockers and bunk frames were dark green, the floor and arching roof a liverish gray, and there were narrow windows along the sides, like gill openings which gave one the sense of having been swallowed, like Jonah.

When enough men are crowded into the belly of a whale, certain things are bound to happen and the smart thing for a newcomer to do is to dummy up until he knows what it's going to be.

Like everyone else beginning a new career, I was determined to make good and consequently I was in practice to be tough.

To be tough was a science I'd learned something about at Interdom. The first rule is to remain as uncommunicative as possible among strangers and the second is to regard everyone as a stranger. When these rules are followed, conversation becomes a series of guttural grunts, nods and signals which enable people to get along like hogs in a tight pen. However, there are two exceptions to this rule about staying dummied up: booze and women.

Booze and women.

Unfortunately, having been institutionalized most of my life I had had no experience in either category. While other boys had been improving themselves in taverns with B girls, taxi dancers and the like I had been absorbed in bookish joys, reading Thomas Wolfe and Melville; in short, wasting my life. But I didn't realize until I was hanging Whistler's Mother on my locker door how this lack of practical experience was likely to affect my standing as a Marine.

Coming into the hut I had noticed four men seated around one of the bunks in close conversation. They'd glanced in my direction resentfully and one of them groaned, but they had gone back to their talk with a kind of secretive eagerness which caught my attention.

"Man, man, man!" one of them said.

"Then wha'd she do, Max?"

"She give me a lesson in geography."

Throaty chuckles.

"Come on, Laperuta, give us the scoop."

The man thus addressed, Laperuta, Corporal Max Laperuta, had a big muscular face, heavy lips, smoky eyes and a grand appearance of satiation. He was describing a sexual exploit and his manner of delivery was powerful. The blunt, descriptive words slipping through his teeth and his hands weaving, patting, plumping and squeezing the air as he spoke, materialized naked ladies right before the eyes of his breathless audience. He was a natural leader of men.

It struck me then that a tough, eighteen-year-old virgin male Marine is something of a contradiction in terms and I was just considering the relationship of continence to my chances for advancement when we were ordered into the street with full packs and rifles.

The men turned out struggling into their gear, rifle butts clattering on the street as they fell into formation. I found my place with the replacements at the head of the column under Strand's watchful eyes. We fell silent and we waited with growing tension as though for a portentous omen; then our commanding officer, Colonel Haskell Pollard, appeared.

I say Pollard "appeared" to distinguish a characteristic of the colonel's. The ordinary man arrives and departs; he comes in and goes out; he opens a door and enters; he leaves and closes the door behind him. Not so the colonel. He appeared. How this was accomplished I cannot say; whether temporarily blinded by awe of his rank and reputation we missed his comings and goings, or whether there actually was some magic in it I can't say. All I know is that the colonel appeared or he disappeared. It was uncanny.

Pollard was a short, wiry-looking gentleman in his early fifties. His face was small, nut brown, with tufted jet-black eyebrows over eyes so light blue that the pupils were nearly lost in the white. He carried a swagger stick covered in morocco leather with a Turk's head knot around a gold Marine emblem at the butt and a thirty-caliber bullet on the tip.

He stood looking at us, his replacements, with a keen,

icy stare and the only sound was the swagger stick snapping his right trouser cuff. *Swip, swop, swip, swop.*

Presently Pollard nodded at Strand. "Let's go," he said, and with that he turned and marched down Basilone Road toward Horno Ridge. He never looked back.

The officers began to holler. The sergeants passed the orders and we followed the colonel, who marched along with Strand half a step behind him. The colonel's metronomic swagger stick ticked his pants cuff in a cadence that set his walking pace at a steady four miles an hour.

It took half an hour for the shock to wear off. Some of the replacements had forgotten their cartridge belts, some wore helmet liners, while others had caps. Clearly we were the dregs of the outfit and this was some kind of test.

As I hoofed along in the dust raised by the men up ahead I wondered what would have happened if the company hadn't followed Colonel Pollard. I got a picture of him marching straight down to the ocean. I saw him cross the dunes to the tide mark, saw him march unhesitatingly into the water until it closed over his head and there was nothing left on the surface to mark his passing but an overseas cap and his swagger stick.

After an hour the column began to settle down. The sun was up and hot. Somewhere an artillery battery was firing a practice mission and the concussion shook the warm air like jelly. We turned off on the Horno Ridge Road and marched into the hills. The dust was terrible. Looking back I couldn't see the men, but I could hear their hacking coughs trailing back half a mile.

We marched three hours with no stop, then Sergeant

Strand jogged up to the head of the column. We'd come twelve miles but Strand showed no sign of wear. He bit the wet end off his cigar, threw the tip away and wadded the remainder down in his jaw with his parrot tongue. Then he began ordering the men to square away. He marched backward booming a cadence count. "One, toop, threep, foa! Pick it up! Come on! This ain't route step! You pogey bait gyrenes are going to be walking on your knees when the sun goes down. Let's hear it! In cadence count!"

"One, two, three, four," we responded listlessly.

"Oh," Strand rumbled, his voice packed with irony. "Oh, that's splendid. You're all sopranos. One, toop, threep, foa, to your lef, right, lef! You people who make it back alive are goin' to have athlete's foot up to your eyebrows. Now let's hear it! In cadence count!"

"One, toop, threep, foa!" we yelled.

"In cadence count!"

"ONE, TOOP, THREEP, FOA!"

"That's better," Strand grumbled then he went down the line kneading and mashing the column into marching order. He straightened the files and got the men in step. He plucked several men whose packs, or dress, or manner of marching offended his eye and sent them to the rear. "Here, you in there," he'd yell, "you, dog meat! You with the two left feet, the short leg and the dumb face; you there, fall out and get back to the ass end. Yes, you! All right, you go with him too, fatso. Not you, stupid. In cadence count!"

"ONE, TOOP, THREEP, FOA!" the men hollered.

"All right," Strand bellowed. "All right, keep in step. I'll send a road scraper through to cover the goof balls and ass-draggin' dope-offs that don't make it. We'll get rid of the fats right now. In cadence count!"

Half an hour and two miles later we came into a field and Strand drew us up in formation.

When the dust settled we saw Colonel Pollard seated on a tree stump tapping the ground with his swagger stick, looking as fresh as when he started. He scanned our ranks and we all felt chastened by his frosty eyes.

"Hitler lives," some goon whispered. "Pass it on."

Colonel Pollard rose and swopped the cuff on his trouser leg a couple of times. The artillery had completed its fire mission; a light breeze died and even the birds fell silent. The colonel looked at the ranks blocked out in front of him. The company officers gathered behind the colonel watched him as one man. He advanced three steps, planted his feet and put his hands behind his back. He bent forward slightly as he spoke; he didn't shout, but his rasping voice honed the words to a fighting edge.

"Men," he said, "First Battalion, 16th Marines, is a go outfit. We go. We go farther, we go faster, we go on our feet and we go to fight. H and S Company is the pace-setter for this battalion and I set the pace for this company. If you new men can't keep up I want to know about it today. The best get-acquainted offer I know is a walk. That's what this has been. Fifty foot-miles a day is what we're going to travel about two times a week, so if any of you are too fat to make it this is the time to cop out. All right, take five."

We broke formation, stacked our rifles and flopped.

I found myself next to one of the men in my hut, Corporal Padgett Powell, a dapper fellow who looked as though he'd descended from a long line of southern plantation overseers. There was a note of genteel cruelty in his manner as he offered me a cigarette which I dared not refuse. Down the line I saw Corporal Laperuta, surrounded once more by a rooting section which included the two other men I'd noticed in the hut, Private Lou Weller, a big Wisconsin boy who shambled around like he was still carrying two pails full of milk, and Private Al Morgan from Jersey, a knuckle cracker with a frozen smirk on his face who just about tasted every word Laperuta said.

I asked Powell about Laperuta and was informed that Max was the greatest Marine in the company, that he'd laid more dames than I could shake a stick at. I didn't miss the equation of sexual experience to greatness, and was wondering how I was going to make up my deficiency in this respect when my attention was attracted by a disreputable-looking carryall which was driven onto the field. "What's that?" I asked.

"That's the Fat Wagon," Powell said. "In this outfit anything that's sloppy, useless or dumb is called fat. Everything that's right is go. That's why they call this the Fats and Go Battalion."

"Fats and Go," I said.

"You'll see."

Before I could learn more we were on our feet and headed back to camp. It was a grueling march—a shakedown cruise, the Old Man called it—and it shook eighteen of the replacements out of the company. Blisters, heat prostration and plain exhaustion dropped them by the road and they were picked up by the Fat Wagon trailing the column.

When we reached Las Pulgas, Strand held us at attention as the Fat Wagon cruised slowly down the face of the formation with its load of misery.

"Let's hear it for the fats," Strand bellowed, and a yell rose from our ranks: "Go, fats, go!"

It was a ritual rejection and it made me think of my mother who must have often wished me away as her girth expanded, and my sympathy went with the fats.

When we broke I asked Powell where the fats went.

"Captain Crowell gets them over in A Company," he said. "Yeah, Crowell gets all the fats."

Like Interdom, I thought and I was determined not to be rejected again.

From then on that's how it was. For H and S Company the wheel had not been invented. The colonel did his staff work on foot at the head of the column. Conferences were ambulatory. Papers he was required to sign reached Division Headquarters dust-flecked or rain-blotched, depending on the weather. The colonel juggled company commanders and gave them maximum authority; if one of them made a requisition he had to answer four questions: Why do we need it? Who carries it? Who eats it? Who shoots it?

When anything rated the Old Man's disapproval he called it "fat." A squad leader reprimanding one of his men would yell: "Hey, fat, where were you when they passed out the brains?" or a platoon sergeant: "All right, you fats! The next time you hear fall in, fall in!" A dirty rifle was "fat." A sloppy pack was a "fat pack."

On those occasions when our performance pleased him the colonel would say: "That's go," and we were happy.

Fats and Go. That's who we were—the leanest, walkingest, meanest Marine Battalion in history.

Two

MEN tend to invent what they need and haven't got; Marines are no exception and at night after the movie was over and before lights out was a very inventive time.

Out of the mouths of all those stranded Quonset whales at Las Pulgas, there issued forth steamy talk of women; it rose into the cool air and hovered over the camp like a great cloud in the shape of a common bawd. She was huge. She was a composite of all the imagined exploits of a thousand men. She was all the movie queens, all the girls next door, all the high school sweethearts, all the pin-up inflations, all the breasts, buttocks, bellies, thighs and faces ever seen, touched, or imagined by deprived males. She was the common feast of night dreams, the big female in the sky.

Max Laperuta was the greatest contributor to this cloud. With Powell, Morgan and Weller listening avidly Max would relate his experiences in Oceanside, our nearest liberty town, while I lurked about petrified that one of them would ask me if I had a girl, or had had a girl.

At night I huddled in my blankets and in my dreams I heard Laperuta's mocking voice and saw his accusing finger under my nose as he made a public accusation that I was a virgin. Sometimes I would start awake, bolt upright in my bunk.

Leprosy would have been acceptable, even a little romantic, but virginity was a crime none of the men could forgive me. They'd turn their backs, smirk, snicker and crack wise. I'd be ruined; the belled virgin of the battalion, the goat, last man in the pecking order.

Virgins are not leaders of men.

To avoid ruin I had to act and being reasonably certain that a lot of the talk was fictitious I decided to invent a girl as a form of self-protection. This seemed eminently suitable because orphans are good at inventing people. They have highly developed creative powers. Orphans, for instance, create their mothers, a singular act entirely at variance with normal reproductive procedures. Occasionally they create their fathers too, but not often.

At Interdom we could frequently tell a great deal about a boy by the kind of mother he bore. Actresses who couldn't acknowledge their maternity without ruining their careers were fairly common. One boy claimed a Congresswoman, another an anthropologist of international reputation who couldn't keep him because she traveled in primitive company and had peculiar notions about cannibalism and the institution of marriage. One boy's mother was an aviatrix who had crashed before she could pick him up at the will-hold desk in the maternity hospital.

The stories were frequently wild, but an abandoned child is often bitter and the imaginative lengths to which he will go to excuse the conduct of his parents is a measure of his charity toward them.

For my part, I went to the St. Louis telephone book one day and under Danbom I found Betty and Clifton H., and adopted them for my parents.

The story I made up for them was sad but admirable.

Clifton H. Danbom was a civilian pilot engaged in surveillance flights over a friendly country. One sunny afternoon while flying at thirty thousand feet, cameras and engines working smoothly, he was shot down, or up, depending on how I was feeling about him that day. At any rate his body was never found.

His wife, Betty, my dear mother, made a claim against the government for support but she agreed to forego it when a State Department representative explained that to admit the existence of Clifton H. Danbom would increase international tensions. So for patriotic reasons Betty Danbom decided to abandon me, the only living proof of Clifton H.'s existence.

When I left Interdom I was given evidence which tended to discredit my idealization of Betty and Clifton H., but the story served me well while I was there and whenever I see a telephone directory I still think of that small, dark, intense woman who sacrificed so much for her country.

I think the telephone book meant more than the Bible to

most of us at Interdom because telephone books are not full of begats. The Bible on the other hand stresses genealogy and for those who don't have any this is a discomfort. But the clergymen who had us in their charge felt impelled to read the Bible at us. Eden, the Ark, the Flood, Jacob and his brethren, Abraham and all the rest of it were swallowed up in begats which are like a spit in the eye to an orphan.

The whole Bible was begat and begetting and we were unbegotten. Maybe the idea was to give us a sense of kinship, to graft us, as it were, to the Biblical family tree, but the grafting didn't take.

We were reasonably certain that our parents hadn't been named Shem, Elam, Hul, Gether or Mash. Maybe if there had been a few Bills and a Jean or two we could have attached our branches to that tree, but Gomer, Javan and Milcah make a hard trunk.

The telephone book is better.

At any rate having invented parents, I thought it would be no great trick to invent a girl.

I called on my creative powers. Night and day I tried to imagine my girl. I thought of nothing else. I made lists of the qualities Laperuta had given his girls and eliminated them from mine. Gradually she began to take shape. I began to see her. Pretty soon I had a girl different from anything Laperuta had described and I decided to give her a test run.

One night I waited until Laperuta wasn't in the hut and tried her out on Powell, Morgan and Weller.

The girl I invented lived in Escondido, a town inland about twenty miles. She had a car of her own. Her parents were wealthy. My girl wanted to give me presents, but I refused them. Morgan asked me why and I said she'd already given me the greatest gift a girl can bestow. That went over fine. Powell nodded solemnly.

But I could tell something was wrong. My girl lacked authenticity or perhaps my tentative delivery failed to give her a proper foothold in the imaginations of the men.

"What's her name?" Weller asked.

"I'd be crazy to tell you, wouldn't I," I said.

He shrugged. "Yeah, maybe," he said in a manner that left no doubt that my initial overture had failed.

Part of my problem was that having given birth to a mother, I naturally had a tender regard for the female sex. I couldn't describe a woman in an earthy way because I didn't have Laperuta's tactile vocabulary, or his experience. Also I was afraid of failure. I knew that I had one chance to make my girl stick. If I failed, everyone would guess my condition and my chance of joining the ranks of the natural leaders of men would be lost.

I contemplated a legitimate approach to the problem: that of resorting to girls of ill repute and thus curing my disability. But I discarded this plan because I was naturally fastidious, not overwhelmingly attractive, and very poorly heeled. I excused myself on the cost factor. Also, in order to defeat Laperuta, it was necessary to have an alliance of a more or less permanent nature. Laperuta was making out every night, to hear him tell it; therefore I had to at least match his time, if not beat it.

I wracked my brains, embellished my creation—who was very unlike my mother indeed, as it turned out—but still she lacked verisimilitude.

When Laperuta began referring to me as "that mother-loving Danbom," I knew my time was running out. I doubled my efforts. While he and the boys went to Oceanside on liberty I repaired to the library where I read such works as *The Kinsey Report*, *Lady Chatterley's Lover* and *Tropic of Cancer*. None of these met my requirements and in desperation I turned, at last, to the Bible which fell open in my hand to the Song of Solomon, where I read the phrase from Chapter One, verse three: "thy name is as ointment poured forth, therefore do the virgins love thee."

I read on gathering riches from that great book, my senses reeling under the fruity impact of pomegranates, apples, grapey breasts, honey mouths and wheat-like bellies set about with lilies. I read the Song of Solomon four times, committing it to memory, reveling in the poetry of it and when at last I was satiated I put it reverently aside, aware at last that parts of the Bible are better than the telephone book. There is not one begat in the Song of Solomon, but they hadn't read it to us orphans.

The next time I talked to the boys I had a description of the Girl from Escondido. I knew her intimately. The joints of her thighs *were* like jewels, the work of the hands of a cunning workman. Her belly was like a heap of wheat set about with lilies; she had breasts like grapes; a honey mouth and the stature of a palm tree. I felt her, deeply. She was my beloved, my sister, my spouse and I was hers.

I saw a light in Weller's eye.

"Man!" Morgan said.

"Boy, I'd sure like to see her!" Powell said.

"Not a chance," I said and I retired victorious, a full-fledged virgin male Marine liar.

During the next few weeks the boys were eager to hear

me talk and Laperuta began to notice their lack of attentiveness. To hold their interest he increased his outside activities.

What had started out on my side as a simple impulse toward equality had taken on serious proportions.

It was escalated coxmanship.

Laperuta countered every Biblical image I recruited with a new sexual escapade of his own. Our struggle got so fierce that he forced me out of the Song of Solomon into the third and fourth chapters of Isaiah. I would have gone through the whole Bible if I'd had to, but Laperuta gave up in Lamentations. By then he was haggard, pale and listless and I thought he had screwed himself out of the company.

He staggered in one night and fell on his bunk. "Three times two," he groaned. "Two, three times—"

The boys and I waited for his explanation.

"Dotty and Alma, three times each," he said. He rolled over on his elbow and looked at us. "I can get an affadavit! No kidding, fellas." His eyes sought approval, but Weller and Morgan chopped him down.

"I seen those broads," Weller said, "they got statures like fat cactuses."

"And the roofs of their mouths is like ashtrays," Morgan said.

Laperuta glanced in my direction with a murderous glint in his eye and for a moment I thought the issue was going to be settled with fists, but he was already too weak. He fell back on his bunk with a terrible moan and from that time on we heard no more from Max Laperuta about women and I was the acknowledged coxman of the hut.

I discovered, however, that lying isn't a lazy man's occupation. One has to work at it. When I started lying I didn't realize how much of my time it was going to take. Source material is fine, but one has to account for his activities, which made me appreciate my hereditary connection, through my father, with espionage.

If I went to Oceanside I had to wear dark glasses and keep my collar turned up for fear of being discovered alone when I was supposed to be with the Girl from Escondido. Frequently I stayed clear of town, spending the liberty hours alone on the beach inventing new episodes to hold the attention of my hut mates. I got to be as lonely and furtive as a criminal.

Sometimes I slipped into Oceanside after dark and ducked into the Palomar or the Star theatres and watched a guts and glory action film, just to have a place to sit down. I sat in the last row with my back against the wall, my collar up, my dark glasses on, listening to the gunfire from the screen and watching the dodging figures.

During this period I fought through Tarawa, Iwo Jima, Bataan and all the hedge rows of Europe. I saw slaughter at the Alamo and I saw Indian legions crumble. It got me.

Most times I sat through the mayhem twice, waiting for the streets outside to clear so I wouldn't be seen by some agent who could report me to Laperuta. At two o'clock in the morning I'd leave the all-night theatre and walk down Hill Street with the ready excuse that I'd just left my girl, in case I was challenged.

I'd pass the no down payment, no carrying charges, no previous credit required direct diamond importer jewelry stores and stop to stare at the ice in the windows, wondering if I ought to buy a diamond for my girl. That's how far my thinking had gone. I could show the installment book to Laperuta and maybe he'd give her more credit.

I stayed clear of the U.S.O. at Third and Tremont, scuttling down the alley to reach the esplanade which ran along the beach, passing signs for bait, tackle, beach supplies, bloodworms and back rests.

I had never been so lonely in my life.

As an example of my dedication to deception I met a cocker spaniel dog one night. It was lying in front of a little motel on the beach front and I approached quite innocently until I was close enough to pounce in the best commando tradition and tear a few hairs from its golden tail. The dog ran off, growling with outrage, but the hairs were a great success.

I put them on my shoulder when I came back to the hut and Weller saw them at once. "Hair from the Girl from Escondido!" he cried.

A tussle developed between Morgan and Weller for possession of these few strands of hair. Weller got a bloody nose, but he also got the hair which he curled into his wallet and kept as a memento which he was frequently called upon to show after one of my descriptions of a vineyard tryst. "Show us the hair, Weller," one of the boys would say and Weller would bring out his wallet.

I began, stupidly, to feel that my future in the Marine Corps was guaranteed by the Song of Solomon and the hair of a cocker spaniel. Of course I had no freedom. I couldn't be seen alone. I couldn't go bowling with the boys because I had to be with my girl. But such are the sacrifices one makes for a career.

Then one night, having slipped into the movie, I was

stricken by a surfeit of guts and glory. Too many bodies had fallen. I was full of death on the silver screen in both black and white and color. And although it was dangerously early I staggered out of my seat at the Palomar and dove for the door with the rattle of Sten guns in my ears. I had probably seen half a million people die on the screen since I'd been going with the Girl from Escondido and all that blood and mortality was beginning to shake me up.

When I reached the street I saw signs on the light post: DROP ANCHOR IN OCEANSIDE. I saw the spinning lights and thought I was going to pass out. I braced myself against the wall, my body wracked with guts and glory. Machine guns, automatic rifles and burp guns were rattling in my skull. I looked at my watch; it was ten o'clock. I raised my dark glasses and scanned the street.

Powell, Morgan and Weller were coming toward me and it was too late to run.

"Hey, Danbom!"

They gathered around. The smell of buttered popcorn from the theatre was terrible.

"Thought you had a date," Powell said.

"Going to meet her in twenty minutes," I lied.

"Hey!" Weller cawed. "She coming by here?"

"No," I said.

"How about you introduce us?" Morgan asked.

"Butt out," I said.

"What kind of car she drive?" Weller asked.

"Plymouth convertible," I said.

Powell frowned. "I thought you said a Buick once."

"What's the difference?" I demanded.

"About four hundred bucks," Powell said.

"We wait here and we'll see her, huh?" Weller asked.

I was on the brink of giving up, but the thought of Laperuta's face stopped me.

"See you guys at camp," I said.

I pushed away from the wall and walked drunkenly down the street. At the corner I looked back. They were arguing with each other. Weller wanted to follow.

I ducked around the corner, ran down the alley and hid behind some garbage cans in back of a café that smelled of country-fried chicken, spaghetti and worse. I sat there waiting for the coast to clear, wishing I'd invented a girl who lived in San Francisco and could only visit me once a month, so I could have been seen in public once in awhile. I was miserable. The garbage cans were full and oozing onto the brick pavement. A cat came and looked at me, its yellow eyes filled with contempt.

I began to think that the cans were filled with all the guts spilled in the movies I'd seen and it made me sick. I peeked over the top of one, half expecting to find Powell, Weller and Morgan standing guard at the end of the alley. Instead I saw a girl. She was standing in a dark doorway, one hand raised toward me and a pleasant smile on her wholesome face. My heart skipped and I raised my dark glasses.

She was cardboard, a manikin for an airline with a sign on her belly which said: FLY NOW; PAY LATER.

I stood up and sneaked down the alley, brushing the manikin which fell over as I passed. At the end of the alley

I looked both ways down the street. Powell, Weller and Morgan weren't in sight, so I hurried toward the beach to get some fresh air.

At the edge of the tide line I stopped and listened to the breakers grumble over the wet sand. Off to my right I could see the Oceanside Pier thrusting out into the water and the lights from the restaurant where the fisherman went for coffee and beer and where couples sat in the booths holding hands while the floor, supported by pilings, rocked gently under them.

I couldn't go there. Not me. I was out with the Girl from Escondido, and she was out with me. Somewhere we were doing it together, but not in bed. We couldn't do it in bed because Laperuta always did it in bed and my girl was different from Laperuta's girls. We did it in the lawn swing at the miniature golf course in La Jolla and in an orchard of pomegranates, with pleasant fruits; spikenard and saffron; calamus and cinnamon; with trees of frankincense; myrrh and aloes. We did it upon the mountains and skipping upon the hills; she raised me up under the apple tree and in the vineyards beneath the clusters of the vine.

We'd exhausted Solomon long ago, but the boys were insatiable. I'd transferred their interest from the act itself to the setting, but this required detail and my inventive powers were sorely taxed.

I considered the fishpools in Heshbon and decided the next episode would occur in a swimming pool, but I was too lonely to think about it. The cardboard manikin had hurt me. The wild hope that she was real and my bitter disappointment that she was not, hurt. She had illuminated my isolation and mocked me behind my fortress of garbage cans. She was more real than my mother or the Girl from Escondido. It was terrible.

Despite the risk of discovery I was drawn toward the pier, to the real people walking there. I climbed the stairs to the ramp and joined the crowds, but I felt like cardboard. It was awful. I watched closely to see if anyone noticed how flat I was. I began to feel that there was nothing painted on my backside—that it was just blank, brown.

I stopped and looked down at the inky swells running toward the beach. The pier shifted under my feet like a ship. My throat ached. I thought I was going to cry, but I was afraid the tears would wash my cardboard face away so I turned my back on the running sea and cursed.

Then, through my dark glasses, I saw a creature walking toward me along the pier, a creature in white or I wouldn't have seen her at all. It was a girl in a pleated skirt with a sweater over her shoulders, with long blond hair in a pony tail down her back. I took my dark glasses off and she was still there. A real girl.

She passed me. I couldn't see her face anymore, just the bobbing pony tail refracting moonlight.

My heart slapped and squirmed like a fish in a creel and I followed her.

She turned down the esplanade, past the playground, past the seafront motels, moving on under the lights.

I saw her turn into a motel down the block. It was a collection of frame cabins with shed roof between them to accommodate the cars—an old-fashioned place, but freshly painted, making a stab at staying alive. There were white-washed rocks edging the paths and each cabin had a name: one was the *Nimitz*, another the *Halsey*, the *Mitscher*, the *Spruance*. The cabins were all named after Admirals of bygone days. It was called the Admiral Motel.

My girl vanished. I couldn't see her anywhere. I went to the office and rang the tap bell on the desk. The proprietor came out; he was short, wiry, forty-five with a little red mustache. He wore the uniform of a chief petty officer, electronics specialist, and he had a pipe wrench in his hand.

"Yeah?" he said, not friendly.

"I'd like a room," I said.

"Full up," he said.

"I didn't see a light in *Nimitz*," I said.

"They're asleep," he said.

Then over his shoulder I saw the girl I'd followed.

She was seated in the little living room beyond the door which the chief had left ajar. She bit into an apple, deliciously, and picked up a copy of *Life* Magazine. There was a cocker spaniel curled up at her feet, the very cocker from which I had gathered hair from the Girl from Escondido. It looked up at me and barked and the chief pulled the door shut.

"You run this place?" I asked.

"Yeah," the chief said, "me and my niece and we don't put up Marines. Now shove."

His niece.

I looked at the chief, incredulous. They were related—he and my girl. They had a listing in the telephone directory. The Admiral Motel. My girl had a place. She had an uncle in the Navy. "This is a very nice motel, sir," I said.

The chief hefted the pipe wrench in his hand. He watched me, waiting.

"Lot of work around a place like this I expect."

The chief's neck was turning red, swelling under his collar.

"What I wanted the room for, Chief, was for my mother," I said.

"Mother?" he said.

"She's coming to visit me from St. Louis and I thought this would be a nice place for her to stay. It's homey. She likes things homey."

"Your mother," he said.

"Mrs. Danbom," I said. "I'm her son, Charles."

"That's nice," he said.

"She asked me to get her a place."

The chief put the pipe wrench down. "When do you expect her?"

"Oh, any time," I said. "Any time."

"I don't make reservations for any time."

"Well, I'm not just sure," I said.

"Oh, not just sure," the chief said. "All right, when your mother comes have her call. If I have a cabin it's hers."

"I'll have her call," I said.

"I'll stay right by the phone," the chief said.

"Mrs. Danbom," I said. "Tell your niece too. Mrs. Danbom."

"Mrs. Danbom," the chief said. "I'll remember."

He picked up the wrench again, measured the gap and screwed it down to fit a half-inch pipe. I stood there watching, and he looked up abruptly. "Anything else?" he asked.

"No," I said. "I guess that's all, thank you." I backed out the door, went to town and caught a bus to the base.

When I came in the boys were playing poker with Laperuta.

"You're back early," Morgan said.

I crossed to my bunk and sat down, ignoring them.

"Tell us about it, Danbom," Weller said.

"Deal," Laperuta said irritably. "It's your deal!"

The boys expected me to come on with another installment of my true story adventure romance and I could see if I hit the brakes there'd be trouble. I couldn't just kill the Girl from Escondido. I had to taper her off. I began to think of fatal diseases she could get like tuberculosis in the operas.

"So what happened?" Powell asked.

"Her car broke down," I said. "Had to get towed clear in from San Juan Capistrano. Any you guys ever had a dame in the back seat of a car that's being towed by a wrecker?"

Weller threw his cards down. So did Powell and Morgan.

"Man!" Weller said.

"That old red light was flashing on the wrecker," I said, "and there she was looking up at me with the front end hoisted and the car kind of dipping up and down on the end of the chain."

"Crazy," Morgan said. "All the way from San Juan Capistrano?"

"All the way," I said. "Her long brown hair was spread out over the seat cushion, and her blue eyes—"

"Short hair, blond," Weller said frowning.

"She let it grow and dyed it," I amended hastily.

"Brown eyes," Powell said.

"In that light they were blue," I said. "The red light, see?"

"Red and blue make green," Laperuta said.

"Green then," I said.

"You said brown before," Laperuta said. "Brown eyes."

"She hasn't been feeling so well lately," I said. "The accident kind of jarred her up some. She was coughing . . ."

"What accident?" Laperuta demanded. "You said the car broke down."

"Well, yeah, but when we ran into the ditch she bumped her head, aggravating her tuberculosis."

"What!"

"That's why she bought the car. She's going to a sanitarium in New Mexico for the rest cure. So there we were and the old Dodge swinging us back and forth on the wrecker chain and that red light blinking."

"Man," Weller said. "Man!"

"Plymouth!" Laperuta declared. "Plymouth convertible. He got up and came to me, his fist closed. "Danbom," he said softly, "you ain't got no girl in Escondido."

"She turned the Plymouth in," I said. "Turned it in on a new Dodge."

"A new car that breaks down the first time out?" Morgan asked.

"So it broke down!" I cried. "Can't a car break down?"

"You're a damned liar, Danbom," Laperuta said.

I bolted to my feet and Laperuta backed off making room to fight.

"The car broke down," I said. "Whether you like it or not, that's what happened."

"He's lying," Laperuta said and they all looked at me.

I snatched a towel from the foot of my bunk and glared at Laperuta. "You say whatever you want, Max," I said. "Her Dodge had a bad transmission; she's got bad lungs and Weller's got a lock of her hair. Show him, Weller." I wrapped the towel around my neck and made for the door as Weller reached for his wallet.

I went down the street to the shower hut and slammed the door behind me. The odor of wet soap, mildew and after-shaving lotion was strong. A couple of men were in the shower room, soaping themselves and singing above the noise of the spray. I went to a washbowl and pretended to wash my face, waiting for them to leave. There were old razor blades on the lip of the bowl and a squeezed-out tube of toothpaste.

I felt cut up and squeezed out. Laperuta had gathered enough strength to mount another attack and he'd thrown me back. If I'd developed the fishpools-in-Heshbon routine I might have been safe, but because of the girl at the Admiral Motel I had neglected my homework. I should have known better than to lie off the cuff; it takes preparation.

I assessed my tactical situation and realized that I had to keep the Girl from Escondido alive until I could produce a real girl to take her place. I even saw an advantage in not killing her at all. I could tell the boys that I'd tossed her over for something better and that she'd flown to Europe to mend her shattered heart.

But they were on to me. I'd seen skepticism in Weller's

eyes and if he had begun to lose faith in the hair in his wallet I knew the others would not be far behind. Stern action was required.

The men in the shower came out. They hailed me and asked about the Girl from Escondido. I put them off with a few words about transmission trouble, stripped out of my clothes and went to take a shower.

As the water beat my face I had the sinking feeling that Biblical images and cocker hair were not going to save me. Like a foolish commander I had failed to take the factors of attrition and obsolesence into account and now Laperuta was at my throat, or rather, at the throat of the Girl from Escondido.

I had lost the offensive and now I needed a new weapon simply to defend my position. It was a hard tactical lesson.

I scrubbed my chest and armpits wracking my brain for a definitive way to put an end to this contest; then I remembered my real girl and how the apple snapped when she bit it. I remembered the sudden whiteness of the flesh as she removed the apple from her lips and she was Eve and the apple was from Eden: The day ye eat thereof, then your eyes shall be opened, and ye shall be as gods, knowing good and evil. Genesis!

I was seized by a triumphant, wretched inspiration, one so blindingly simple that without hesitation I turned my face and bit my shoulder.

I bit my shoulder very hard.

I nearly drew blood, but a sound caught my attention and turning around, I found Sergeant Strand staring at me in pop-eyed astonishment. A green towel covered part of his scaly nakedness. A cigar stub was stuck in his face and he held a black bar of Lava soap in one hairy hand. He looked at the teeth marks on my shoulder, then met my eyes.

"There any insanity in your family, Danbom?" he asked.

"I don't know, Sarge," I croaked. "I'm an orphan."

Strand nodded dubiously. "An orphan," he said, "a crazy orphan. You need someone to look after you, Danbom."

"I can look out for myself," I said.

A batrachian smile crossed Strand's face. "I worry about you, boy," he said. "I think I've found a place for you in this man's outfit."

"I'm doing fine," I said.

"Yeah? Well, from now on you're the chaplain's assistant. In the morning you take the Fat Wagon over to Division Supply and pick them up. Three chaplains: Hallowell, Horowitz and Duff."

"Chaplain's assistant!"

"That's right. The T.O. calls for one and you're it."

"But Strand! I'm allergic to the clergy!"

"Are you happy in the Corps?"

"I'm an atheist!"

"Dig a foxhole!"

"But we got one chaplain! Chaplain Bernard!"

"We got three more."

"That's fat!"

"You're telling me? The Old Man nearly broke his swagger stick, but there's nothing he can do. They're Navy Reserves on the base for a six weeks' summer cruise. Division assigned these three to us. Your job is going to be to keep them out of the colonel's line of vision. You understand?"

"Strand, please! I'm a low moral type. You know my reputation."

"Yeah—which is why I like you for the job. You might get uplifted. On the other hand, if those three Bible bangers bother the Old Man, I'm going to restrict you to the base and you'll never see that tart of yours."

"Strand!"

"It's done, Danbom. Now shut up. Put them in that hut closest to the hill and move your gear over there in the morning."

"I got to live with them too?"

"For as long as you're likely to live, yeah."

"Sarge," I begged, "have a heart."

"I have never had any use for one," he said.

"Can't we make a deal?"

Sergeant Major Strand put his hands on his rumpless hips and tipped toward me until his nose nearly touched mine. "Danbom," he rumbled, "I don't make deals. I'm sergeant major in this outfit, get me. You're dandruff, Danbom. You're an itch in the crotch. You're a pick in the nose, get me?"

I nodded.

"You're a bug in the ear," Strand continued. "You're stale sweat. You slither. When I spit you wipe. When I bark you jump. When I belch you salute—get me?"

Tobacco spittle punctuated his remarks and I got him.

"You're a brown stain, Danbom. And you're the new chaplain's assistant of this outfit. Wiggle, crawl, squirm or weasel, that's what you are. Now repeat after me: I am the chaplain's assistant."

"I am the chaplain's assistant."

"I promise to do my duty to God and my country and if the fat chaplains bug the Old Man to cut their throats."

I repeated it.

Strand's little rhinocerine eyes held me fast for one red moment; then he nodded. "That's the deal," he said, "now haul ass out of here."

I returned to the hut a much chastened man and as the lights went out I knew how Adam felt when the gates of Eden closed behind him.

As a chaplain's assistant I saw little hope of preserving my reputation as a tough, two-fisted Marine and I lay awake remembering my years of misery at Interdom, the loaves of raisin bread and the black coffee which constituted our penitential breakfast on Sunday morning, the hole in the staircase leading to the dormitory which was supposed to have been left by a bullet fired at a Chinese lunatic who had tried to sneak upstairs to collect flesh for his chop suey with a butcher knife.

But most of all I remembered Brother Queen with the razor strop under his cassock and rimless glasses which glittered so that his eyes were always hidden as he read us *The Hound of Heaven:*

> "Still with unhurrying chase,
> And unperturbed pace,
> Deliberate speed, majestic instancy,
> Came the following Feet.
> And a voice above their beat—
> 'Naught shelters thee, who wilt not shelter Me.' "

Brother Queen's sepulchral voice and the content of the poem scared us more than the thought of the Chinese madman who had come to butcher us in our sleep. We often dreamed of hounds tearing at our souls and at night the little ones would frequently wake up gasping, their faces white with dread.

When, at last, I fell asleep the hounds were baying: "Hallowell, Horowitz, Duff!" And one of them with ember eyes had his fangs fastened in my shoulder and was dragging me down in the midst of the ravening pack.

In the morning I examined my shoulder. It was blotched and purple but the teeth marks were plainly visible.

Powell saw the bite. "Christ, Danbom!" he said. "What happened to your shoulder?"

I hesitated just an instant, then I plunged: "She bit me. The tow truck hit a bump and she bit me," I said.

Powell's face went blank and I knew how Lincoln felt when his audience hadn't responded to the Gettysburg Address.

"Clear through your shirt?" he asked.

"I had it off."

Weller moved over to look at the bite. "Good glory, look at them teeth marks," he said.

"Man!" Morgan whispered, his eyes fastened on the bite. "Man, man!"

And before I could interpret the situation I was overwhelmed. Weller threw his head back and crowed: "She's real, goddamnit! I knew it. I knew it! I'm going to put that hair of hers in plastic!"

Men clamored to see the bite on my shoulder and even

mistook some of the bruises I received in their pummeling enthusiasm for further evidence that the Girl from Escondido was an athletic lover. Emboldened by this success I announced that I was to be the chaplain's assistant, which brought howls of laughter. The fact that the greatest coxman in the Company was going to be the chaplain's assistant was almost too much for the men to bear. Morgan rolled on the floor. "An effing chaplain's assistant!" he gasped.

Laperuta watched these antics with a deep scowl on his simian face. He was brooding.

"I still say you're a liar, Danbom," he grumbled.

"Well, Max," I said, "there's about three hundred men in this outfit who believe me. You're the exception. However, I am and have always been willing to accept the judgment of a majority of my peers. It's the democratic way."

As I left the hut Laperuta told me what I could do, but I pointed out it was not only impossible, but unnecessary since I had a girl in Escondido.

Three

BEFORE I got the Fat Wagon to transport the three Hounds of Heaven who had scented me out, I looked up the number of the Admiral Motel whose proprietor was listed as Edwin S. Budd.

I dialed the number and got the chief.

"Is this the Admiral Motel speaking?" I asked.

"No, this is Chief Budd speaking; the Admiral Motel don't speak." The chief chuckled and I knew him at once for a wit.

"This is Charles Danbom," I said.

"Oh yes," he said.

"Remember me? I came in the other night about a room for my mother."

"I remember," he said.

"I was wondering," I said and I took a deep breath, "I was wondering if I could speak to your niece—Miss Budd."

"No," he said. Just like that. "No."

"Well, Chief," I said, "I think you ought at least to . . ."

"And I don't care where your mother stays. I had a hunch about you, Danbom."

"You've got me wrong, Chief," I said. "I'm a chaplain's assistant."

He hung up, bang—in my ear.

I decided to swallow my pride and dropped another dime in the slot ready to apologize to the chief for being disconnected, but my courage failed so I got my dime back, boarded the Fat Wagon and drove over to Division Supply.

When I backed up to the freight dock at the side of the building, a supply sergeant came out pushing a hand truck loaded with cartons and crates. "You're going to be full up," he said.

"What's all that?"

"Standard issue for chaplains according to Fleet Marine Force regulations," he said and he recited the article. "Regimental chaplains are to maintain a full supply of consumable, non-perishable church equipment ready at all times for embarkation. This includes: one thousand New Testaments," the Sergeant hoisted two crates from the stack on the truck and put them on the dock, "five hundred Protestant prayer books, five hundred Catholic missals, five hundred rosaries, two hundred field hymnbooks and one portable field organ."

"You're bulling me," I said, staring at the heap of boxes.

"I'll get the organ," the sergeant said.

"Two hundred field hymnbooks?"

"That's the regulation, buddy," the sergeant said. "Song and Service Book for Ship and Field."

"Come on, Sarge, I'm not hauling this crap back to Pulgas."

"They're your chaplains," the sergeant said and as he pushed his truck into the warehouse, Chaplains Hallowell, Horowitz and Duff appeared in the doorway.

They were dressed in officers' khaki. Dressed? They occupied it. They stood there, cinching their belts, tying their field scarves, affixing collar tabs and bars. They were lieutenants.

Over in the Zulu impact area an artillery battery cracked a salute; the shells eggbeat the air and hit seconds later with a dull whump. The chaplains looked around, saw me and smiled.

At Interdom, I'd been exposed to all kinds of clergymen, but never three at once who were so much all kinds of clergymen. They stood there, short, tall, fat, dark, light, ruddy; three sets of different colored eyes looking at me, and I couldn't be sure any two eyes of one color were in the same head. Their features shimmered in the heat waves rising round them; one smiled, one frowned, one looked perplexed.

I saluted crisply. "Sir, I'm Pfc. Charles Danbom, chaplain's assistant, H and S Company, First Battalion, 16th Marines, reporting," I said.

They saluted and one of them introduced the triumvirate.

"I'm Chaplain Hallowell," he said, "and this is Chaplain Horowitz and Chaplain Duff."

"Glad to meet you, Chaplains," I said and I began to load the carryall. They pitched right in to help me.

Gradually I began to sort them out. It was hard, like separating the three monkeys, Hear no, See no, Speak no evil, or Father, Son and Holy Ghost. They were a trinity like Neapolitan ice cream.

None of them was over thirty, but one was boyish, the other avuncular and the third careworn.

The boyish one was Hallowell, Frederic Hallowell, or Freddie. One of the chaplains called him Freddie, the other Frederic.

Freddie, or Frederic, Hallowell weighed about a hundred and sixty pounds.

The short one, the rotund, kind of Friar Tuck one, the rubicund and hearty one, weighed about a hundred and sixty too, so by weight they were nearly the same but set up differently.

That made three hundred and twenty.

The long dark one, the Don Quixote, would go a hundred and seventy-five, but on him it looked skinny.

His name was Nathan Horowitz; he had Tablets of the Ten Commandments with a Star of David on his collar.

Duff was a Catholic.

Hallowell, Horowitz and Duff. Protestant, Jewish, Catholic; young, avuncular, careworn; medium, chubby, lanky; fair, rosy, dark; one-sixty, one-sixty, one-seventy-five.

Four hundred and ninety-five pounds of assorted fat. Little wonder Colonel Pollard had nearly broken his swagger stick.

As Chaplain Horowitz read the labels on the crates he began to express some agitation. "One thousand New

Testaments," he said. "Five hundred Catholic missals?" His expression darkened.

"What's wrong, Nathan?" Chaplain Hallowell asked.

Horowitz reared up, his face stormy. He glowered at Hallowell and Duff. "Where is the Torah?" he demanded.

"What?" Duff said.

"One thousand New Testaments, five hundred Catholic missals, where's the Torah?" Horowitz repeated darkly.

"Certainly they must have something for you," Chaplain Duff said and he began searching through the boxes.

"No," Horowitz declared. "Nothing."

"They'll adjust that," Hallowell said.

"Adjust it!" Horowitz cried. "Adjust? Not one Talmud! Not one Siddur! Two hundred hymnbooks, but no Rashi, no Maimonides. The Jews are the People of the Book and what do I get? Nothing. What do you get? Everything. Goyim!"

Duff tried to placate Horowitz, patting him on the shoulder. "I'll share mine with you, Nathan," he said.

"Share!" Horowitz bawled. "How can a rebbe work with these shmates? Look!" Horowitz pointed a shaking finger at the field organ the sergeant wheeled out on the hand truck. "Musical instruments, you get. Do I get a violin? No! A piccolo? No!"

"You can use the organ," Duff said.

Horowitz roared.

The supply sergeant, dumfounded, stopped in his tracks and Horowitz advanced on him.

"Tell me, Sergeant," he said sweetly, "do you have a shofar in your warehouse, a little ram's horn?"

The sergeant looked at me, then at Duff and Hallowell as he retreated before Horowitz.

"Have you a few hundred mezuzoth tucked away, or a tallith?"

The sergeant's eyes sought me imploringly.

"Maybe in a corner somewhere," Horowitz said with menacing kindness, "you'll find a few gross yarmolkes, or a dusty menorah?" Horowitz stopped and pointed at the heap of boxes on the dock. "Are there no Jews in the Marine Corps?" he cried.

"Of course there are," Hallowell said.

"Don't contradict me!" Horowitz bellowed. "How do I make a minyan?"

"Nathan, I was agreeing with you," Hallowell pointed out.

"He was agreeing with you," Duff said.

"There, you see," Horowitz cried pointing from Duff to Hallowell. "*Tzorress* and *tzvilling* rarely come single."

When we'd finished loading, Chaplain Hallowell put an alligator suitcase in the front seat. "Don't want to crush it," he said, "my sheet music is in here. Choral arrangements, a pitch pipe and my baton. Do you sing?" he asked.

"No, sir," I said, "I do not sing."

"Very good for morale," Hallowell said. "I had a remarkable boys' chorus in my church in Detroit."

"That's nice, sir," I said.

With all the crates and the organ in the car there wasn't much room, but the chaplains climbed in. Chaplain Horowitz perched cross-legged on a crate of New Testaments in the front seat. Chaplains Hallowell and Duff were in back with the organ and the rest of the boxes.

"Cheerio, Fats and Go," the supply sergeant called.

"Funny as hell, Sarge," I said bitterly.

The road back to camp was rough and each time we hit a chuck hole the field organ perched between Chaplains Duff and Hallowell gave off a disgusting sigh, which Hallowell said was B flat.

I noticed Chaplain Horowitz eying me speculatively. He said my name several times under his breath, savoring it. "Danbom," he said, "Danbom."

He studied me for a time, then asked if my mother was Jewish.

I explained I didn't know who my parents were and this encouraged him.

"You could be Jewish," he said.

"I don't think so. Is Danbom a Jewish name?"

"Is Horowitz? What's in a name?"

"I don't think I'm Jewish," I said.

"Are you sure?"

The organ let off a terrible wheeze.

Chaplain Hallowell began to hum a tune and I sighed. "All right," I said. "All right, I'm Jewish."

Chaplain Horowitz looked at me, startled. His eyebrows elevated. "That's strange," he said, "you don't look Jewish."

Any illusions I might have had that these chaplains had found me by accident vanished in that moment. They had come for me and it wasn't a question of placating them, no, they were going to thresh me for my soul.

Chaplain Hallowell broke into song; he had a rich, uninhibited tenor voice and I could have strangled him. "Where have all the flowers gone?" he sang. "Long time passing. Where have all the flowers gone? Long time ago."

We passed the Horno Rifle Range where a platoon from the Second Infantry Training Regiment was firing on targets in the butts. Their rifles spanked the air like paddles hitting water and the chaplains leaned out to watch.

"Real bullets, I expect," Chaplain Hallowell said.

I decided to test them with a bit of obfuscation. "Only those that hit the target, sir," I said.

They looked at me, solemnly.

"Very good answer," Chaplain Horowitz said after some deliberation. "Very good."

"Come on, Nathan," Chaplain Duff said, "the other bullets are also real. A bullet is just a lump of lead whether it hits the target or not."

"A lump of lead, maybe, but not a bullet," Horowitz said. "A bullet hits the target."

"A bullet is a bullet when you put it in the breach of a rifle, Nathan," Chaplain Hallowell said.

"No, that's a cartridge," Horowitz said.

Chaplain Duff chuckled. "Got you there, Frederic, that's a cartridge."

The chaplains' voices rose excitedly and their hands began to weave in front of them as they argued.

"A bullet is born at the muzzle of the gun," Chaplain Duff said.

"In the breach at the instant of explosion," Hallowell said.

"Still a lump of lead until it hits the target," Horowitz said heavily. "Our knowledge of the bullet comes from our knowledge of the target. A bullet describes a trajectory in time. We know its genesis, but to know the bullet we must also know its terminus."

"You say: 'The bullet hit the rock.' Of course you do," Duff said.

"I infer the bullet from the rock," Horowitz said.

"You're also inferring the rifle," Hallowell said.

"I heard a shot and from that inferred the rifle. If I hear no shot and see no rock I infer no bullet. I infer a lump of lead."

"Common sense, man!" Duff cried. "Every bullet hits something."

"A fishing sinker is a lump of lead," Hallowell said. "Is it a bullet?"

"When a fishing sinker is shot from a gun and hits a target it is a bullet," Horowitz said. "Only then."

"A fishing sinker is a fishing sinker!" Duff cried.

"We used split shot for fishing sinkers sometimes," Hallowell said placatingly.

"Split shot are irrelevant," Duff declared testily. "I'm trying to make Horowitz admit that all bullets are bullets. Nothing is more obvious."

"Nothing is more mistaken," Horowitz said doggedly. "Are all men Christians at the muzzle?"

"What?" Duff asked. "What?"

"Of course not. So a bullet misses its target is a lump of lead. Danbom is right."

"Let it go, Duff," Hallowell advised.

"He doesn't even know what a common bullet is!" Duff wailed. "A common bullet! Maybe he wouldn't know a dumdum bullet, a soft-nose bullet, an explosive, or an expanding bullet, but a common bullet? Is that so confusing? A simple projectile?"

"Tell me, my friend," Horowitz said calmly, "you fire a rifle in the air, the bullet lands you know not where. What is it?"

"What is what?" Hallowell asked.

"A bullet! A bullet!" Duff insisted.

"By whose report?" Horowitz asked.

"By the rifle's report?" Hallowell asked.

"By the report of whoever finds it," Duff said.

"No one finds it," Horowitz said.

"There is objective reality in the sight of God," Duff cried.

"To my God it is a lump of lead," Horowitz said with finality. "Unless, of course, it hits the target, whereupon it becomes a bullet. Transubstantiation."

"Madness," Duff moaned and they lapsed into silence with their arms folded over their chests.

I turned on Basilone Road headed for Las Pulgas. After their argument petered out there was a momentous silence. I felt the heat of their attention growing and I knew that I, Charles Danbom seated at the wheel, represented a theological vacuum each of them felt obligated to fill. For a brief, panic-stricken moment I thought of driving off the road, of sending myself and this load of fat anomalies hurtling to our deaths, but the recollection of my real girl spared us. I hadn't even met her, but already she'd saved my life and the lives of three assorted chaplains.

I drove on slowly as the urge to self-destruction dampened in my breast and gratitude for the existence of my savior welled up.

Presently the chaplains in the back seat leaned forward with their arms crossed. Their eyes tickled the short hair on the back of my neck and I knew it was coming. A quiz. I tried to squinch down inside myself. How many times had I gone through it as a boy?

Who made us?

God made us.

What is the Fourth Commandment, son?

Honor thy father and thy mother, sir.

What is the corporal? The corporal is a linen cloth on which the Host and Chalice rest. Have you learned your verse today, Charles? Yes, sir. Recite it for us, please. "Unto every one that hath shall be given, and he shall have abundance; but from him that hath not shall be taken away even that which he hath."

That's very good, Charles, and how do you interpret that verse?

He that has gets, sir. Well, now, Charles, I think you've misconstrued the meaning of that particular passage, don't you?

Seems clear to me, sir: he that has gets.

"How long have you been in the Marine Corps, Danbom?" Hallowell asked.

"Six months, sir," I said.

"Do you enjoy it?"

"Yes, sir," I said. "It's a wonderland."

"And what brought you in?"

"A recruiting poster, sir," I said.

"A recruiting poster?"

"Yes, sir, outside a post office in St. Louis. It was standing there with a Marine on it, looking at me over his shoulder with a smile on his face, beckoning me to follow. I followed and that's how I got into the Marine Corps."

"Is that how they get Marines?"

"No, sir. Most of them come in to avoid the Universal Military Service and Training Act as amended."

"How's that?"

"Well, sir, if you're drafted you might end up in the Army, Navy, Air Force or Coast Guard. Marines usually volunteer. That way they avoid being drafted."

"I see."

"Marines are some smarter than the average serviceman," I said. "They come in here and get free food, free housing, free clothes, free training and get paid on top of it. It's like Socialism."

The chaplains thought about this. They sat back. They pondered heavily whether or not to make the distinction for me between socialism and military necessity. I had hoped they'd attempt to do so for by this ruse I would have lured them out of the swamps of theology into the quicksands of politics where I could have engaged them, soul free, for months.

Unfortunately they must have sensed the bait for they didn't rise to it and we drove on in armed silence until we came to the Santa Margarita bayonet course. A platoon of sweating, dust-caked Marines were running at dummies, charge, parry, thrust, retrieve. Their bayonets flashed in the sun and the men hollered as they ran at the dummies, sank their bayonets and grunted: "Aagh!"

I stopped the Fat Wagon. "Here's an example of the training we go through," I said. The chaplains turned to watch. "Those long knives on the ends of the rifles are called bayonets. The stuffed canvas dummies on the posts represent human beings. Some of the men imagine the dummies to be armed males of military age, but most of us like to think of them as old ladies, or officers.

"Old ladies?" Duff said, dismayed. "Surely not old ladies!"

"Oh, yes, sir," I said. "I've often heard a man come back and say, 'See how I stuck that Old Lady there?' "

"Heavens!" Duff said.

"Yes, sir," I said. "You see, sir, it's an exercise in broadening the imagination, of evoking one's creative powers, of venting the hostilities which impede the flow of our deepest, truest thoughts."

A Marine ran through the course, howling as he stabbed the sawdust-dribbling dummies.

"Now watch this man," I said. "See how he runs. See his rifle held high. Hear him cry out as he swivels his way through the hail of fire which he imagines to be directed at him. Now he jumps, plants his feet. See the concentration as he parries the wooden stake. Now, ah! See how he sinks his bayonet. Three inches, slight twist, retrieve, and on he goes. That's theatre."

The three chaplains stared at the sawdust dummy, a great slashed hole where its belly should have been.

They were impressed.

"It's an exercise which engages the whole man," I continued. "He has to sink the bayonet just three inches or run the danger of getting it fouled in gut or bone, which means he'd have to jerk free with his foot on the opponent's chest, and in that time he might get a bayonet himself.

"There, he's gone through without missing a dummy. Look at that trail of slashes and gashes. He's coming back. See the look of gratification on his face. The rifle hangs in his hand. He smiles, breathing heavily. He looks back at the slashed dummies and that's all they are to him now, just dummies, but what were they as he ran? Who were they? See how he smiles."

The chaplains were silent.

"Corporal Danbom?" Hallowell said presently.

"Yes, sir?" I said.

"You have a very vivid imagination."

"Got it on the bayonet course, sir," I said.

"What faith were you raised in, son?" Chaplain Duff asked.

I knew it had been coming. I'd hoped that my description of the bayonet course would cause them to forget ecclesiology, but there it was point-blank.

"What's that, sir?" I asked, stalling for time.

"I asked what is your faith," Duff said.

"Well, sir," I said, "to tell you the truth, sir, on my religious preference card it says: 'Declines to state.' "

"Declines to state," Horowitz echoed.

"Surely you have some preference," Hallowell said, tipping forward.

"Well," I said, "lately I've been giving it a great deal of thought and I guess I tend toward Unitarianism. It's a good American religion, headquarters in Boston."

"Yes, we know," they said.

I thought for a minute that I'd thrown them off the trail, but no.

"That's good, Danbom," one of them said presently. "You just keep an open mind."

Five minutes later we bounced into the company area and created quite a stir. The organ was wheezing B flat; Chaplains Hallowell, Horowitz and Duff were perched on the mountain of gear. Marines in the area stopped to watch us, mouths agape.

I drove to the Quonset we had been assigned and stopped in a cloud of dust.

"Here's your home," I said.

"Looks like an ark," Horowitz said, "give or take a cubit."

"Yes, sir," I said, "there's room for two of every kind." Then I excused myself to report to Strand.

On the way to headquarters I looked for a rainbow in the sky but there wasn't one anywhere.

Four

I PICKED up the chaplains on Friday, then I had a week-end pass which gave me two days to contemplate my fate, mend my tattered fortune and meet my real girl, the princess of the Admiral Motel.

How to meet her, how to engage her interest, her sympathy, even her slightest attention seemed an insurmountable problem, particularly since she was guarded by her Marino-phobic uncle, the chief.

I really didn't know how to go about it. I had seen many girls, of course, but couldn't remember having spoken to one for any length of time. On one occasion I'd asked a waitress for a hot dog and hold the mustard, but I'd forgotten what she looked like. Then on the train after boot camp I'd bumped into a girl in the aisle and excused myself, but these incidents didn't seem to apply.

I went to Oceanside and took a turn along the beach near the motel, trying to compose things to say but none of them sounded right. My imaginative powers had deserted me and I began to wonder if I was congenitally incapable of facing female reality. I'd already created two imaginary women, my mother and the Girl from Escondido and their hold on me was very strong. In a way Miss Budd threatened their existence.

Mother, it seemed, preferred the Girl from Escondido and her reasons were very convincing.

After all, I was just starting out. There was plenty of time yet to get serious about girls. And what did I know about this one anyway? One apple doesn't make an orchard.

The Girl from Escondido wore an expression of undeserved injury. What had she done to turn me against her? Had she not been faithful, compliant, obliging? Was she not fair to look upon?

I roved the town half hoping one of the boys would find and stop me, but no one did. I returned to the beach and marched along searching the sand for an inspirational pattern, but there was none and I was left wondering how a person so lecherous, so tainted and impure as myself could possibly meet a girl like Chief Budd's niece.

How could I thrust myself into her presence? My position as chaplain's assistant was inadequate to my sins, my reputation condemned me.

When at last I looked up I was astonished to find that it was dark. The sun, like my vain hope of a normal relationship, had gone down. The breakers on the beach wooed and consoled me with voices from the Song of Solomon and the St. Louis telephone directory and it seemed that the Girl from Escondido and my mother had a permanent hold on me.

There was a pale flat moon in the sky exuding madness from every crater on its face. "Danbom!" I said to myself aloud. "Do you want to be cardboard forever?" And I turned and ran down the beach to the Admiral Motel where I posted myself on the stone-edged pathway which led to the office door.

I must have stood there an hour before the door opened and Miss Budd came out carrying a wire milk basket with two bottles rattling in it. "My goodness!" she said. She had a housecoat on, quilted, long to the floor, and one pale hand clutched at the neck. "Well! My goodness," she said and she backed inside, shutting the door.

I stood there straight, at attention.

She looked at me through the curtain. I didn't move.

Presently the door opened and she set the bottles out, quickly, but before she could close the door again I saw a hay-gold streak, heard two frantic barks and then the cocker spaniel from which I'd taken the hair of the Girl from Escondido snapped its teeth into the calf of my left leg.

"Farragut!" Miss Budd cried. "Oh, he's bitten you! Farragut, you bad, bad dog!"

She ran down the path and scooped the excited cocker into her arms and stood there looking at me, her own hay-gold hair tossing and a look of such compassion in her eyes that I nearly fainted with delight. "He's bitten your leg!" she said.

"That's all right, miss," I said. "I've been bitten before."

"But you could get distemper, or something terrible. You'd better come inside. I'll call a doctor."

"I don't think he broke the skin," I said and I followed her up the path with Farragut snapping at me over her shoulder.

"I can't imagine what's gotten into him. He's never bitten anyone before. Are you sure he didn't break the skin?"

We came into the office and she put the dog out and shut the door. "Which one was it?" she asked.

"Which what?"

"Which leg, silly."

I examined my left leg. The teeth marks were barely visible and the skin was whole. "It's nothing," I said.

Miss Budd was relieved. "What were you doing out there anyway?" she asked.

"Well, I came to tell you not to expect my mother. I spoke to your uncle about a reservation for her, but you see I don't have any mother. I lied about that."

"You lied about your mother?" she asked, frowning.

"Yes, I did, I told your uncle she was coming, but she's not. So don't wait for her because she isn't coming. I wanted you to know."

"Oh," she said, kind of funny. "Well, since you're here, the least I can do is offer you some coffee to make up for the bite."

"Thank you very much," I said and I followed her into the living room behind the motel office. It was about eight feet square and full of overstuffed furniture which had seen better days. She brought a pie from the kitchen, told me to take the big chair, then put the pie on the coffee table in front of my knees. She sat cross-legged on the floor and cut two slices. "Loganberry," she said.

She'd made the piecrust herself, not from a mix but from real ingredients, which I thought was significant.

I asked her name.

"Ella," she said. "Ella Budd."

"Ella," I said, "my name is Charles Danbom."

"Charlie?"

"You're the first person who ever called me that," I said. "It's like starting all over again."

"You're crazy," she said.

When the coffee was ready she rose straight from the floor smoothly, her legs hidden in the folds of the quilted robe, and brought the percolator and cups.

While we ate, she told me her uncle had the night duty, that he was stationed at Camp Elliott near Miramar, that he was going to retire in two years and that the motel was his nest egg.

I told her I was a chaplain's assistant.

"Really?" she asked, looking up at me. "How did you get to be that?"

I was tempted to brag, but instead I told her about my religious exposure at Interdom and about being an orphan. "One of the nice things about being an orphan," I said, "is that they don't have any Oedipal complex."

She laughed and I loved her. She thought Oedipal was like edible, so I told her about how orphan boys having no mothers made it easier for them to fall in love with girls.

"You're crazy," she said.

"You're my real rose of Sharon," I said. "You are as a lily among thorns."

She seemed frightened. "You're funny," she said.

I told her I had a weekend pass and asked if I could see her again. She thought about this while we finished the pie.

"You'd better call first," she said. "Uncle Budd doesn't like Marines but if you call first, I could meet you at the Price Rite Drugstore."

I promised to call and as I left she touched my arm, not purposely I think, just the lightest brushing touch as she opened the door, and caught Farragut before he could bite me again.

When I reached the base it was a relief to know that I wasn't going to have to entertain the boys with tales of the Girl from Escondido. I came into the hut and found the chaplains gathered at one end. Chaplain Duff was playing Bach on the little Estey portable field organ. Chaplain Hallowell was studying his sheet music and Chaplain Horowitz was poring over the Torah. It was a peaceful scene, a much better atmosphere in which to contemplate Ella and I began to think that perhaps my association with the chaplains was going to prove beneficial. I even began to think kindly of the chaplains and I decided not to do unto them as I would unto other Marines.

In the morning I called Ella. I got Chief Budd.

"Is that you, Danbom?"

"Chaplain's Assistant Danbom speaking," I said cheerfully.

"Don't give me that crap. I know what you're after."

"Chief, my intentions are honorable."

"Anybody'd lie about their mother would lie about anything. You come around here again and I'll brain you!"

"Please, sir, let me talk to Ella."

"Drop dead, Danbom!"

He hung up.

I calculated Ella would have heard the chief's final outraged yell so she would know I'd called. Thinking she might go to the Price Rite, I looked up the number, waited five minutes and called the Admiral Motel again to check. I got the chief.

"Is that you, Danbom?" he cried. "You yellow creep, answer me! If I catch you around here again I'll rake gravel with your face, you hear me, Danbom!"

I muffled the phone. "This is Arthur Hollisher, arrangements chairman for the Southern California Kiwanis convention," I said.

Budd wasn't sure.

"I'm calling from San Diego. Would you be able to put up twelve delegates on the week of April 5th? I'm canvassing for accommodations and I'll have to know at once."

I could hear Budd rustling the calendar on the desk. "Just a moment, Mr. Hollisher," he said. "Yes, I'm sure we can put up twelve of your delegates that week. If you'll just send me a telegram to confirm, I'll hold the space."

"Hold your breath also," I said.

"Danbom! You slithering, white-bellied leech, you maggot, you toad's stool, donkey dung bastard . . ."

From his language, I concluded Ella wasn't there. I hung up and called the Price Rite. The phone rang forever. Finally it was answered.

"Yeah?" The voice was a man's, impatient and testy.

"Sir," I said. "This is Charles Danbom, a Marine at Camp Pendleton. Sir, would you please just look over at the fountain and see if there's a girl seated there."

"There's four girls seated there and a little boy with a dog," the man said.

"Sir, if it wouldn't be asking too much could you just call over to the fountain and see if one of the girls you see there is Ella Budd?"

"Ella Budd!" the man called.

I waited. "Sir?"

"They all turned around including the little boy and his dog. The dog is growling."

"Sir, please, is the dog a cocker spaniel named Farragut?"

"No it's a bulldog. He's coming this way. Mean-looking cuss. Scary."

"Sir, if you close the door on the booth the bulldog won't bother you."

"Glad you thought of that," the man said and I heard the door of the booth close. "Damned thing is standing out there growling at me," he said. "What did you say your name was?"

"Danbom, sir," I said.

"Thanks, you may have saved me from a nasty bite. Never get along with dogs. Used to be a postman. Always nip me."

"Sir, about this girl. Could you try again?"

"Door is closed," he said. "The bulldog is watching me. Kid is eating a fudge sundae. Just started. So you're a Marine, eh, Danbom? I was in the Army myself, Rainbow Division. Ever hear of it?"

"Yes, sir."

"Grand outfit, grand. Should have kept right on going, yes, sir! On to Moscow!"

"Moscow?—Which war was that, sir?"

"Nineteen-eighteen, what else? That was a war! None of this hanky-panky technical stuff. Fighting! Cold steel, hot lead, trenches, mud. Over the top! Yes, sir! Through the wire."

"Sir, please."

"Gas!" he said. "Mustard gas! Weren't afraid to use it then."

"Sir, about the dog?"

He subsided. "Dog? Oh, dog. Yes. Glad you thought to close the door."

"Sir, are the girls still there?"

"I'll have a look, wait a minute."

I heard him thrash around in the booth to take a look. I heard a dog bark.

"Yell her name, sir. Ella Budd."

"Ella Budd!" he yelled. "Ella Budd!"

The bulldog was yawping. I could hear it jumping against the door. There was a crash. I waited. I whistled into the phone to attract someone's attention. "Hello?"

It was Ella. "Charlie, is that you?"

"It's me," I said.

"My uncle had no right to yell at you the way he did," she said.

"I'm afraid your uncle and I are never going to hit it off too well," I said.

"It's like the Montagues and the Capulets," she said with a pretty sigh.

She was full of surprises like that.

We arranged to meet on the beach and an hour later we

were running across the sand with a blanket and a picnic basket and I was hooting at the sea gulls which rose into the sky and flapped away over the breakers.

We found a hollow in a sand dune and flopped down, laughing. It was warm and we were alone and we began to talk like it was going out of style. I told her about the begats and Benny Cohen, which she thought was awfully sad. She told me about her mother who'd run off to Orlando, Florida, with a siding salesman and how she'd decided to stay and help her uncle with the motel. Her father was dead so she was about as orphaned as I was.

"Marry me," I said.

"I've never been asked to before," she said.

"If you don't I'll die unmourned."

"Do I have to marry you to mourn you?"

"It would be nice."

She smiled. "Since when are you going to die?"

"Since I was born."

We ate the lunch—cream soda, dill pickles and egg salad sandwiches—and after awhile Ella said she had to cook dinner for the chief. For my money she could have let him starve, but she said he was going down to Miramar and I could come after supper.

After she went home I lurked around town for awhile and ran into Weller.

"Hey, Danbom," he cried lunging out the door of the bowling alley, "how's she going?"

"She's going to New Mexico next week," I said.

"Ah, no!" He was disappointed.

"Yeah," I said.

"Ah, no. I don't believe it."

His lack of credulity irritated me. "I said she was going to New Mexico."

"I can't believe it," he said. "What are we going to do?"

"What do you mean what are *we* going to do? She's my girl."

"I need her," Weller said dismally. "I couldn't get along without her."

"I'm sorry as hell, Weller," I said, "but she's going to New Mexico for her lungs."

"No kidding!"

"You wouldn't want her to die, would you?"

"I guess not, but I can't believe she'd leave you."

"As a matter of fact I was getting bored with her anyway," I said. "All that sleeping around in orchards and vineyards and on mountaintops was getting me down. I could never get her indoors."

"Maybe she needed the fresh air for her lungs," Weller said.

I nodded. "That could be."

"The best girl I ever had was in a haymow," Weller said.

"Yeah, well, she's leaving next week."

"You're going to write to her, aren't you?"

"What's the use?"

"That's a lousy thing," Weller said. "The least you could do is write."

"All right, I'll write."

"You owe her that much," Weller insisted. "I wrote the girl I had in the haymow, but she never answered."

"Too bad," I said.

"She got braces on her teeth. I guess that's why."

"What?"

"It improved her appearance, so she never wrote."

"That's too bad," I said.

"I could tell right off your girl didn't have no braces."

"Tuberculosis," I said.

Weller nodded. "It's always something," he said sadly. "If it ain't braces or tuberculosis they get knocked up."

"Yeah," I said, "ain't it the truth. Well, I got to shove." I left Weller, his big face wreathed in woe, and walked down to the pier where I could see the Admiral Motel.

The chief drove a 1950 Ford pickup which had an arsenal of tools in the back. He used it to get to Miramar, to haul gravel for his driveways, boulders to edge his paths and lumber to repair his roofs and porches.

When I saw the chief drive away, I walked down to meet Ella and found her waiting for me on the porch.

"Let's sit out here, Charlie," she said, "it's nice."

She patted a place at her side and I sat down. We listened to the waves and watched people passing along the esplanade. Some kids were screeching about having to go home and throwing sand in each other's eyes. An old couple came along, helping each other, talking memories. The lights began to come on in the houses and along the streets and it was good to be just sitting there.

"What are you thinking about?" Ella asked.

"Oh, nothing," I said.

She looked at me gravely. "Charlie," she said, "if you're a baby when they find you and they don't know who you are, how do you get a name?"

I'd never told anyone the truth about my name. The ordinary person, even with a name like Terwilliger, Snook, or Lerchenmueller, might, on occasion, feel defensive about it, but they have the support of their ancestors who bore the name before them, whereas I had not.

Juliet was right to complain so much about a name. When I discovered the derivation of mine it pretty nearly killed my mother. The story, delivered to me as I left Interdom for the larger world, made me question not only her existence, but her patriotism.

Ella frowned a bit and shook her head solemnly. "You don't have to tell me, Charlie," she said, "and I'll never tell another living soul."

"Well," I said, "when they found me there was a note that said: 'My baby's name is Charles. His father is a damn bum.' They changed damn bum to Danbom."

"Oh, Charlie," she said with such a lot of breath behind the words that it scared me.

"I'll change it," I said quickly. "You can have whatever name you want: Rockefeller, Kennedy, Eisenhower, Johnson."

"I'll keep Danbom," Ella said quietly and she tipped forward and kissed me on the cheek.

I couldn't remember having been kissed before. There had been no kissing at Interdom and none at Parris Island; perhaps in my infancy I'd been kissed, but the sensation had vanished long ago and now Ella's kiss, so soft and brushing in front of my ear, almost made me believe in fairies. I sat there full of wonder, and overwhelmed by a sense of loss for all the time I'd wasted reading books.

"Haven't you ever had a girl before?" Ella asked me.

"No," I said, "not ever. The only thing I ever had was a chipmunk in a cage at Interdom."

She looked at me tentatively and I thought she thought I was lying.

"His name was Harold," I said. "I fed him sunflower seeds."

"Everybody has to have somebody," she said presently.

I nodded.

"Maybe I could be your girl," she said.

"I wish you would," I said.

It was quiet except for the breakers on the beach and time seemed to occupy the night air, warm and flossy as cotton, and the streetlights down the esplanade shed a softer light on the figures passing there like a dream.

"All right, I will," Ella said.

And I began to wonder if any of it was real. I looked at Ella and she was there in three dimensions. I took her hand which was firm and alive. The tide was going out and there were radio waves all around us carrying terribly awful, corny, romantic love songs and the television sets in all the houses were tuned to terribly awful, corny, romantic love stories. It was love at first sight. I would never let her go. I'd die for her. We were happy.

"What are you thinking about, Charlie?" Ella asked.

"I'm happy," I said.

"So am I."

"How does happiness feel to you?" I asked.

"Nice," she said. "Do you want to play some Chinese checkers?"

I said sure and we went inside, but we didn't play. Ella got the board and the marbles, but before she could set them up I pulled her down on my lap in the big chair. She wasn't pomegranates, spikenard or apples, or cinnamon, myrrh and aloes, she was Ella and when she ran her finger along the bridge of my nose and kissed me again I knew she was real.

"Marry me," I said.

"Charlie, you're crazy."

"I do the best I can for one of Whistler's Mother's boys," I said.

And I told her how the boys at Interdom always gave a print of Whistler's Mother to the guys who left. It was a traditional gag, but she thought it was sad. "You've had a sad life, Charlie," she said.

"It's taken a turn for the better," I said. "I've got a girl and a home in the Corps. What more can a man ask?" And I promptly asked to see her the next afternoon.

She looked sorry. "I promised to help my uncle paper *Nimitz*," she said. "So I can't."

"What happened to *Nimitz?*"

She sighed and snuggled down. "Somebody opened a bottle of warm beer and shot it all over the walls."

We sat there until it was time for me to catch the last bus back to the base. I asked if she wouldn't try to get her uncle to come to chapel one time. "If he saw me in action as a chaplain's assistant maybe he'd soften up toward me," I said.

Ella said she'd try and after one more kiss I left hating the guy who'd splattered the beer in *Nimitz* for robbing me of an afternoon with my girl.

Five

ON Sunday morning the chaplains were up and frisking about bright and early.

After breakfast we boarded the Fat Wagon and drove to the base chapel where Chaplain Bernard delivered one of his nondenominational sermons to the chaplains who were on the base for their summer reserve cruise. There were about forty of them, as pious and motley a crew as anyone could imagine.

Chaplain Bernard, our base chaplain, was a bluff, rather pompous major. Through the week he was ordinarily very saving of speech, but on Sunday his sermons were studded with aphorisms he'd collected or concocted during the incubation period from Monday to Saturday. "Let him among you who has never sinned throw the first grenade." . . . "The Lord is on watch with you. Call on Him. If He answers, demand the password."

It was inspirational.

After the service Bernard read the chaplains their training schedule including such items as graves registration, hospital evacuation procedure and field sanitation. He made it clear, however, that the place of the chaplains was with the men of the outfit to which they had been assigned. "We're here to serve God and men in the field. We go to them. They don't come to us."

When it was over, Chaplain Bernard drew Hallowell, Horowitz and Duff aside. From his manner, I judged he'd had a certain amount of static from Colonel Pollard. It had been Bernard's idea to divide the chaplains among the outfits on the base. Division had approved but Bernard was probably worried that one battalion commander might infect the others with the notion that the chaplains were an imposition and thereby negate the whole program. Chaplain Bernard led the way to his office and beckoned us inside.

For a moment, Bernard stood with his back to the door, then he cleared his throat and motioned Hallowell, Horowitz and Duff to a seat on the couch in front of his desk. "You too," he said to me, "take a seat."

"Yes, sir," I said.

Chaplain Bernard sat down at his desk, locked his hands in front of him and stared at them. "Orientation," he said thoughtfully.

He glanced up at the three chaplains perched on the edge of the couch. Then he studied his hands again as though they were an intricate Chinese puzzle incapable of solution. He wiggled his thumb experimentally to see if it was the key to releasing his hands, then he frowned and tried his index finger. "Peculiar situation," he said presently.

Bernard wiggled his left ring finger and seemed surprised that it moved. The chaplains were fascinated; Horowitz was about to suggest a solution to the problem, but Bernard pulled his hands apart and threw them up with a sigh. They fell down again, one on each side of his desk blotter. Chaplain Bernard tilted his chair back. "Gentlemen, I'd like you to consider what I'm about to say as privileged; that goes for you too," he said to me.

"Yes, sir," I said.

"Trust breeds trust, I say," Chaplain Bernard said and he cocked his head, appreciating the aptness of this remark which he filed in his Sunday Sermon Index. "Gentlemen, let me put my cards on the table."

"Please do, sir," Chaplain Duff said.

Bernard locked his hands across his chest. For a moment he gazed, enrapt, at the ceiling, then his hands separated with a knuckle-cracking retort which popped him to his feet in a hortatory stance.

"Colonel Pollard is a good man," Bernard said loudly. "I was with him in Korea and, gentlemen, it's sometimes hard for us to estimate the extraordinary pressures brought to bear on a commanding officer. I know for a fact that the colonel has been working around the clock. He's been hammering at Division to put his battalion to the test. So you can see how important it is to Colonel Pollard that all goes well. You *can* see that, can't you?"

The chaplains nodded agreeably.

Chaplain Bernard took a gulp of air. "Very well then.

Now as I say, Colonel Pollard is one of the finest Marine officers I've known. I've known a lot of them and they've known me. We've known each other which makes for an interrelationship, and that's important! Interrelationship.

"Now you men must put yourselves in the way of understanding Colonel Pollard's problems; I don't mean personally in the way of, but intellectually and emotionally. As chaplains, our problem is to understand problems and, as you know, interrelationship is the essence of problems."

Chaplain Bernard pursed his lips and frowned.

"The essence of interrelationship is problems," he repeated, but the meaning of this seemed to have escaped him. "Isn't that right, gentlemen?" he asked.

Horowitz sat forward raising a tutorial finger. "Well, sir," he began—

"That's right, sir," I said loudly. "Exactly right."

Chaplain Bernard swung toward me. "Thank you," he said. "Exactly right. Now, gentlemen," he said, "the thing we have to do is to mesh."

"To mesh?" Chaplain Hallowell asked.

"Yes, mesh," Bernard said and to illustrate he brought his hands together with the fingers bent like cogs; he rotated one hand over the other as he spoke. "We have to mesh our religious principles to the military gear; do you see that? This intermeshing must be smooth, like the interlocking cogs of a well-running machine. A well-running machine, meshing, you see?"

"By its fruits we shall know it," Horowitz said.

Chaplain Bernard looked at Horowitz and forgot his hands, which continued to rotate. "Well, Chaplain Horowitz," he said, "the important thing is not the fruits; the important thing is to avoid friction. The important thing is that we not . . ." At this point Bernard's finger cogs locked, his knuckles cracked and his hands were ground into an expressive lump of bones and flesh. He looked at them.

"Religious meshers?" Hallowell said.

Bernard stared at his hands and abandoned the illustration. He put his hands behind his back. "So much for that," he said. "I'm sure you understand what I mean."

The chaplains nodded dutifully.

Chaplain Bernard returned to his desk and sat down. He placed one hand on the right side of the desk blotter, the other on the left. "Gentlemen," he said, "we're having a little trouble with our image. Colonel Pollard thinks we're fat."

Chaplain Duff glanced at his paunch and sat up straighter.

"That's just a catch-all term, but you must realize that the colonel is a man who believes in the strict separation of Church and State." Chaplain Bernard nodded and went on. "Just so. A fine principle. He does, however, set a good example to the men by attending church services regularly. His daughter makes him come." Bernard smiled self-consciously and cleared his throat as one of his hands began to creep across the blotter toward the other. Bernard slapped it lightly and his hands stuck together.

"Now the reason for this little get-together was to explain these matters to you, so that we understand one another. The point, gentlemen, is that we must be careful not to call too much attention to ourselves. Display lacks humility. I might say, in fact, that it behooves you gentlemen to be humble to the point of invisibility—in a jocular manner of speaking." Chaplain Bernard grinned, not so jocular.

"Now, gentlemen, the colonel is a fair man, a just man, but he's a busy man. However, I know everything will move along just fine if we adopt the old slogan of two Indian tribes who lived on a bordering lake: 'You fish on your side, we fish on our side, nobody fishes in the middle.' " Bernard smiled.

There was a prolonged silence. The chaplains stared at one another and at Chaplain Bernard.

Presently Horowitz lifted his shoulders in a shrug. "Sir," he said, "with that kind of fishing, who's meshing?"

Chaplain Bernard blanched. He stood up. "Gentlemen," he said, "a word to the wise should be sufficient. In your outfit there's such a thing as fat by association. Now, for the good of the group, for the sake of the other chaplains in this program, I'd like you to be . . . ah, careful, circumspect, in short . . ."

"Holy ghosts," Horowitz interjected.

Chaplain Bernard winced, but upon consideration he approved the remark. "Yes," he said, "in a manner of speaking—holy ghosts. But don't haunt Colonel Pollard."

On the way back to Las Pulgas the chaplains were quiet and the Fat Wagon left a cloud of exhaust fumes and smoke behind it as murky as their thoughts.

"We'll have to meet this Colonel Pollard," Duff said. "I'm sure we could win him over. He must have faith in something."

"Firepower," I said.

Presently Chaplain Hallowell pulled a pitch pipe out of his pocket. "Music," he said, "hath charms to soothe the savage breast."

"I wouldn't depend on it, sir," I said.

"We need voices for the choir," Hallowell said.

"I can't sing," I warned.

"Nonsense," Hallowell said, "everyone can sing." He blew his pitch pipe. "Ohh," he sang. "Just repeat that tone in a relaxed manner. Ohh."

"Ohh," I sang.

"Hmmm," Hallowell said. He looked at his pitch pipe.

"Well now," he said brightening, "let's see how long you can sustain one note. Ohhhhhhh."

"OOOHHhhOOoHooO," I sang.

Hallowell studied the pitch pipe thoughtfully. "You have a very unusual voice," he said. He blew another note. "Do you hear that, Danbom?" he asked.

"Certainly, sir."

"Tell me the difference between the first note and the one I've just blown."

"It's thicker, sir."

Hallowell looked surprised. "Thicker?" he said. "Which was thicker?"

"Can't you tell, sir? The second note was thicker than the first."

"Ah, I see," Hallowell said. "Not lower, thicker."

"Lower, sir?"

"The second was lower than the first on the scale."

"The first was thinner," I said.

This was the last musical discussion I ever had with Chaplain Hallowell.

When we reached camp, I left the chaplains to their own devices and spent part of the afternoon trying to resist calling Ella. But the thought of her papering *Nimitz*, with a lock of hair plastered to her forehead with wallpaper paste, was irresistible. I knew Chief Budd was there, but I figured my chances at fifty-fifty and dialed the Admiral Motel. I got the chief.

"Hello, Chief," I said, "this is Charlie Danbom."

I waited for the explosion, but it didn't come. Instead of yelling, Chief Budd's voice was like molasses.

"Aaah," he said. "Ah, yes, Charlie Danbom, the acolyte, the chalice bearer and candle lighter. How is the ministerial assistant today?"

I wished he'd yelled.

"Is Miss Budd there?"

"Charles Danbom, did you say? Where is the spiritual Danbom? We much prefer the spiritual Danbom to the Charles Danbom."

"Chief Budd," I said temperately, "I appreciate your wit; one of the many things we have in common is our enjoyment of laughter."

"So you've been casting your bread upon the waters, eh, Charles?"

"About that call the other day—I realize I overstepped myself, Chief, but I want you to know it was in the spirit of good fellowship."

"Turn two more cheeks and you'll have a quartet, Spiritual," Budd said.

"Chief, I called to ask permission to speak to Miss Budd."

"She ain't here," Budd said.

"Come on, Chief, give me a break. Where is she?"

"I'm sorry I haven't your powers of divination, perhaps I could tell you."

"Chief," I said, "I want to extend you my personal invitation to come to our chapel here on the base next Sunday. You'll enjoy it."

"Not while you're futzing up the clergy I won't."

"Look, Chief," I said. "Will you give Ella a message for me?"

"I'd love to," he said.

"Tell her I called."

"Well, I'll tell you," Budd said. "Ella may be a little slow, she may be a little too trusting, but when she fell for that crap about you consorting with the Bible bangers I knew the end had come. It just don't tally with your Diamond Jim Brady personality."

"Chief!" I cried. "Call Sergeant Strand at the office, 16th Marines. Ask him!"

"I already did. There are no chaplains on the battalion table of organization," Budd said.

"Chief, that's a temporary situation!"

"So was this. Ella went to the movies to think it over."

That night I stared into the arching darkness of the beast which held me and my mind turned with the earth, twisting my spinal cord like a rubber band until it knotted.

My blankets were hot, tangled between my legs. I counted sheep and they turned into clergymen. I drummed a tattoo on the floor with my fingertips and held my breath. I thought of Ella, but the Girl from Escondido was there. Sometimes she came like that and I was ashamed of having plagiarized the Song of Solomon.

I remembered Benny Cohen again. "There are no fairies," I said aloud. "I'm going real, Benny," I said. "I'm going straight. No more pretend, hear me?"

Benny didn't hear me. Mother didn't hear me. The Girl from Escondido didn't hear me. And the chaplains weren't on our table of organization.

Chief Budd had exploited this fact and Ella had doubts which made me realize by what a slender thread I was suspended between the world of imagination and reality. It was gossamer as a hair from Farragut's tail.

"One more thing, Danbom," Chief Budd had said, "you may fool Ella, but you can't fool my dog."

"He already bit me once," I said.

"Yeah, I know, so why ain't you twice shy?"

At last I slept, but now the hounds of heaven were joined by Chief Budd's cocker and they chewed me in my dreams.

At Reveille I found Chaplains Hallowell, Horowitz and Duff dressed and ready at the foot of my bunk.

"We're ready to go," Hallowell said. "Let's be up and doing."

I washed and shaved. The self-inflicted bite wound on my shoulder was still visible and I began to wonder if it was going to be permanent, like the Scarlet Letter.

The chaplains, determined to follow the enlisted men's routine, went to chow at the mess hall where they saw

Colonel Pollard's order to the effect that nobody was to be excused from calisthenics drill. During breakfast, Chaplain Hallowell tried to recruit some voices for his choir but got no takers. Then we went to the drill field and fell in with the men.

There was still a tincture of iodine in the gray morning sky, the fading remnant of a sunrise, and the cool air was sharp in the lungs. We stood there on the tarmac field stamping our feet, stretching our arms, hushed as cattle waiting for the drill instructor to appear. Sergeant Brody of Company headquarters led us in this mild form of torture which had the effect of ramming breakfast down into the lower colon like gun wadding. Brody arrived and hopped up on the platform so we could see and follow his movements. His blouse stretched taut over his muscular chest, he grinned and brought the company to attention. It was a lousy way to start a day.

The chaplains had assured me that they were familiar with the drill, so I wasn't concerned about them. Calisthenics is calisthenics. But as we began I wished I'd asked the chaplains for a rehearsal.

Brody counted smartly as we went through the contortions and I kept a weather eye on the chaplains in the file ahead of me. I noticed Chaplain Horowitz had a windmillish tendency. During the exercise in which you slap your hands over your head and jump your feet together he got out of synchronization. It wasn't bad at first, but presently his big hands began to slap half a beat behind the rest of us; he tried to catch up with his hands and succeeded in doing so, but his feet got out of phase so that he was jumping his feet together when we jumped ours apart. Horowitz tried to correct but failed and presently he began to jerk, hesitate, clap, jump and falter like a scarecrow in a high wind. A pained expression crossed Brody's face. Horowitz' gyrations were infectious; the men around him began to miscount; soon the file behind him was out of phase. Fortunately Brody reached the count of ten before the whole company was contaminated.

Chaplain Duff had trouble with the deep knee bends; one of his legs pushed harder than the other on the rise and as the count increased he developed a kind of hydraulic list which threatened to topple him over on his right ear. Brody watched Duff anxiously, applying body English in an unconscious effort to control Duff's list.

Of the three chaplains, Hallowell was the best coordinated; he ran the series smoothly enough, but halfway through he developed a noisy chuff in his breathing. He began chuffing one to the count, increasing to two, then three. "One," Brody would yell.

"Chuff."

"Two."

"Chuff. Chuff."

"Three."

"Chuff. Chuff. Chuff."

Brody scowled at Hallowell and I began to worry. If, in the course of calisthenics, the chaplains could draw so much attention to themselves, what chance did I have of keeping them out of sight?

We came to the concluding exercise, the push-ups, and the chaplains fell forward with the rest of us. Up, down, up, down, pushing with our arms, belly off the deck.

The count for each exercise was ten and as we approached it I breathed a sigh of relief. I heard Brody yell ten and stood up.

"I believe I can do one more," Duff said. "Blessed Mary, sustain me."

He did another push-up. Hallowell and Horowitz, not to be outdone, also did another. Then, to my dismay, they went on.

"Chaplains," I said urgently, "it's over. You can get up now."

Duff glanced sidelong at Horowitz. "Belly up," he warned.

"You've got more to worry about than I have," Horowitz replied.

"Chu-uff!" Hallowell said and the count went to fifteen.

"Chaplains," I said, "it's finished. Get up. The exercises are over."

They paid no attention.

"*Shma Yisroel. Adonoy eloheynu. Adonoy echod,*" Horowitz mumbled.

"Chuff, chuff."

"In the name of the Father, the Son and the Holy Ghost . . ."

Twenty!

Brody came across the field to watch, amazed.

I tried to get the chaplains' attention again but they were locked in an ecumenical contest and would not give up.

"*Oremus et pro perfidis Judaeis,*" Duff said.

"Don't need your help," Horowitz shot through his clenched teeth.

Twenty-four!

The company broke formation and the men gathered

around the chaplains like iron filings attracted to a magnet. Presently the whole company was watching.

"He is near who justifieth me: who will contend with me?" Horowitz declared.

"*Sicut aqua effusus sum, et disjuncta sunt omnia ossa mea*," Duff prayed.

"Behold, I am causing breath to enter you . . . chuff, chuff . . . I will put sinews on you . . . chuff, chuff. . . . For I shall satisfy the weary, chuff, chuff, spirit, and every drooping spirit I shall have, chuff, filled."

Twenty-six!

Marines who hadn't been inside a church in memory suddenly discovered religious preferences. Before the count had gone to twenty-eight, six hundred and seventy-four dollars had been wagered on the result. They were gambling on the chaplains and Sergeant Brody held the money. Horowitz, because of his size, was heavily favored.

Two Catholics from the Service Platoon exchanged blows, one accusing the other of apostasy for having bet on Chaplain Hallowell.

Some of the men began to pray aloud for their candidates. "Oh, Lord, I got six bucks on his back. Keep him going!"

"*Levate*, Padre! *Levate! Oremus!* You *levate!*"

Other men groaned in martyred agony with each pushup. "Ohhhh!" they groaned. "That's the baby. Ohhh!"

The chaplains pushed and pushed, sweat popping on their flushed faces as the slow, terrible count reached twenty-nine.

At thirty, Hallowell began to lag and Protestants with money on him fell to their knees praying for a new infusion of spiritual strength. "Raise him! oh, please!" they prayed.

Hallowell responded.

Chaplain Duff's short, chunky arms seemed inexhaustible and trinitarian money was going three to one against the monotheists'.

It was eerie. A lot of Marines were on their knees, hands clasped, gazing far-eyed into the sky.

Then, just when it seemed that a great religious question was about to be settled by force of arms, Colonel Pollard appeared.

He appeared as usual. Without notice, he was in our midst, his swagger stick gnashing as he swopped the cuff of his trousers. *Swop! Swipswop!*

There was a nimbus of frosty rage about his head.

"Take him up, Oh Lord!" someone shouted.

"Att—ten—shiun!" Brody bellowed.

We froze.

The three chaplains fell simultaneously. They flopped down, semiconscious, eyes shut, faces white.

Colonel Pollard looked at Strand who came through the crowd; his eyes were dry ice, smoking cold.

He looked down at the prostrate chaplains.

No one moved.

Colonel Pollard gestured at the chaplains with his swagger stick. "I trust," he said quietly, "that presently we shall have a religious awakening," whereupon, as he had come, he disappeared.

When I got to the chaplains' office the phone rang. It was Strand. "You're restricted to the base!" he yelled.

"Sarge!"

"Scratch one week, Dandruff!" he roared. "Those chaplains have ruined the men! Guys all over here are trying to beat their record. Thirty push-ups! One week, Dandruff!" He hung up.

I flopped into a chair, furious at the injustice of it. One week, for thirty push-ups. Hounds of heaven! Without even trying they'd started separating me from the tangible world. Given half a chance they'd drag me off to one heaven or another, but I had one here on earth if I could get to her.

"One week," I moaned. "One awful week." And I wondered how Ella would take the news. I could imagine how Chief Budd would work it over. He didn't even believe the chaplains were real. I groaned and it took all my orphan strength not to be self-pitying.

After the calisthenics the chaplains went to the Field Medical School for a lecture on graves registration. I checked my watch and saw it was time to pick them up so I drove over in the Fat Wagon.

The Naval Hospital was on O'Neill Lake, the only sizable body of water on the base, and it was artificial, but attractive nevertheless with shade trees and picnic areas along the beach. When I got there Chaplains Hallowell and Duff were seated on top of one of the picnic tables in the sun, reading their field manuals. Chaplain Horowitz had crossed the road and was standing over a stake driven in the ground with a crosspiece on it bearing a troop designation and a date: F-2-6 11/18/52. Hallowell hailed Horowitz, who looked around and shook his head indignantly.

"Look here," he said, "look at this! No name, no serial number, nothing! If this is the way they bury a serviceman on a Marine base, what must it be like overseas?"

"Sir," I said, "that is a pit toilet. See the sanitation manual."

"Not graves registration?" Horowitz asked.

"No, sir," I said. "Pit toilet. When they're used up they fill them in and leave a marker."

The chaplains boarded the Fat Wagon without comment.

That night I called the Admiral Motel and got Ella. "Ella!" I said. "It's me, Charlie."

"Charlie who?" she said,

"Charlie Danbom!" I said.

"Oh, yes," she said like she was putting on fingernail polish and had the phone cradled between her shoulder and her ear. Like she didn't care enough to hold it close. Like she was getting ready to go out somewhere.

"How are you?" I asked.

"Very well, thank you."

"Ella, I'd come to see you, but I got restricted."

"I didn't think chaplain's assistants got that," she said.

"Well, they did thirty push-ups and the colonel caught them."

She wanted to know who did thirty push-ups. I told her Hallowell, Horowitz and Duff. She wanted to know how their thirty push-ups got me restricted.

"Well, I made this deal with Strand to keep them out of the Old Man's way."

"Which old man?"

"Our C. O., Colonel Pollard. He thinks they'll contaminate the men and I'm inclined to agree with him."

"I see," she said, but I could tell she didn't.

"Religion and the military don't necessarily mix," I said. "And these are Navy chaplains and the Navy and the Marine Corps don't get along too well either, as your uncle will no doubt tell you."

"He says all Marines are liars."

"Ella, the reason these chaplains aren't on our table of organization is that they're only here temporarily. It's a reserve training program."

"Then you're just a temporary chaplain's assistant," she said.

"That's right."

"You didn't tell me that."

"I didn't think you cared."

"I guess I don't," she said.

I could see I was getting myself in deeper the longer I talked and decided I'd better dummy up until we were together again and she could see my honest face. "Ella, I'll come see you the first chance I get. Maybe Strand will relent a little if the chaplains behave."

"That'll be fine," she said.

"Ella," I said, "I love you. I guess I'd better let you go now."

"So long, Charlie," she said and it was like the telephone company just went out of business. So long Charlie never sounded so final.

I went back to the hut, curled into a ball on my bunk and pulled a blanket over my head.

Thirty push-ups. Their notoriety spread through Fats and Go faster than the fame of my Girl in Escondido, faster than phrases from the Song of Solomon. Men in every company tried to beat that record.

Yes, thirty push-ups was writ very large in Fats and Go. And the conclusion was that there was something in religion after all. The conclusion was that there was an equation of faith to muscularity, or buoyancy, or stamina. The conclusion was that to do thirty push-ups you had to be religious, or that if you could do thirty push-ups you were religious.

With thirty push-ups the chaplains had won the hearts of the men; they were respected, nay, they were loved.

It was awful.

What had started as push-ups bid fair to ruin my relationship to Ella and to buy the Old Man out. There was an underground movement in Fats and Go.

At night, men came to our isolated hut and sang. They sang songs like "Turn Back, O Man" and "Onward, Christian Soldiers"; Hallowell's baton was taking the place of the Old Man's swagger stick. Chaplain Duff's little four-octave organ lured the men into our hut like children to the Pied Piper of Hamelin and all this in two days.

Men who had formerly listened to Laperuta's tales of wench thumpery were sublimating themselves in song. The great bawd of the communal imagination grew scrawny as the chorus swelled. Interest in the Girl from Escondido fell off, not that I minded since she was going to New Mexico anyway, but the moral tone of the battalion was improving so rapidly that all I could see ahead was another week of restriction.

I asked the men to sing softly. I begged Chaplain Hallowell to keep his activities secret. I knew that if Strand discovered what was going on I'd be a prisoner on the base for the rest of my natural life.

Two squads of fats came over from A Company and joined the chorus. Intrabattalion rivalry was in danger of breaking down because the H and S men found that the A Company men could sing as well as any others. Being tone deaf, all I could hear was thick and thin, but it was loud.

At one point, Chaplain Hallowell attempted to incorporate me into his clandestine chorus. "You can be the aspirator, Danbom," he said.

"What's that, sir?" I asked.

"Well, the aspirator controls the breathing of the chorus. He mouths the words without singing them aloud, and when he runs out of breath the conductor knows it's time for the chorus to breathe, you see?"

"I just move my lips, is that it?"

Hallowell nodded. "That's right," he said. "Aspiration is very important."

I could see he was trying to get my support, but I didn't think it would improve my situation with Ella to tell her I was the aspirator in a chorus. I figured I'd about stretched her credulity far enough already. To avoid the aspiration I told Chaplain Hallowell I was short of breath which he understood, being afflicted in the same way himself.

Along toward the middle of the week, Colonel Pollard scheduled a two-day hike with a mock assault on the European combat village. I was relieved because it meant the temporary suspension of choral practice and if nothing went wrong while we were away from camp I hoped Strand would let me have a pass on Monday.

I stuffed my field pack, using an empty candy carton to pad it out, but the chaplains, having had no experience hiking with Fats and Go, packed solid. I tried to warn them about the colonel's swagger stick pace. I told them to travel light, but they'd fallen into the ecumenical trap once again.

For every New Testament Hallowell packed, Horowitz packed the Old, and Duff packed two Catholic missals. They loaded their packs with hymnbooks, tracts, field manuals, Bibles, missals and beads. Horowitz topped his load with a menorah and I had all I could do to dissuade Hallowell from carrying a collapsible music stand. When they'd finished I estimated their packs weighed a hundred and twenty pounds apiece, but each was convinced that his God would sustain him and I didn't feel it was my place to shake their faith. I relied on Colonel Pollard to do that.

Six

THE next morning we started at dawn on a walk that took us into areas where the squirrels had never seen human beings. The only thing that made us sure we hadn't walked out of the twentieth century were the contrails left by jet bombers in the sky, but even these began to look like worm trails on the sweat of our eyeballs.

It was such a walk as packs a man's essence down into the secret hollows of his bones where it hopes to survive, such a walk as puts blisters on his soul that pop and smart and scab over and make him know he has one.

Colonel Pollard didn't walk a step less than the rest of us. He led the way swip swopping with his swagger stick, up hills and into valleys, through territory that could have been Africa, China or Uzbekistan. We couldn't tell and after two hours we were long past caring.

It was a shakedown cruise, but the Old Man shook not one New Testament out of Chaplain Hallowell's pack, not one Talmud, not one missal from the packs carried by Chaplains Horowitz and Duff. It was a shakedown cruise, but the Old Man failed to shake that albatross organ which Chaplain Duff had insisted upon hauling along.

Yes, the organ. Duff insisted. The field regulations stated that the organ was part of the chaplain's field equipment. I pointed out that in a normal outfit there would be transportation for it, but that in this company an organ was fat. One couldn't shoot it and one couldn't eat it, therefore it was fat. Duff said they could carry it, and carry it they did —uphill and down, through brush and grass, woods and water. Horowitz traded off with Hallowell and Hallowell traded off with Duff. After ten miles I took pity on them and joined the organ-toting relay.

"It's no fatter than his fat stick," Duff said at one point. "He can't shoot that swagger stick, or eat it either."

"Fat stick," Horowitz said. "Colonel fat stick."

The roots of my hair went cold. "Not so loud," I said. "A thing like that gets around and the Old Man wouldn't be able to live it down."

"Well it is fat," Hallowell insisted. "That stick is fat by his own definition."

"Rank has its privileges," I said.

But as I thought about it I knew the chaplains were right. The swagger stick was fat and I began to see that the colonel was only human after all. Heretofore I'd thought of him as a demi-god, which is the proper attitude of privates toward their commanding officers, but "fat stick Pollard" stuck in my mind. It was one of those catch phrases which have the power to destroy, like "land reform," or "freedom now." It could be devastating.

At Division they already referred to us as the Fats and Go Battalion and it was a miracle to me that someone up there hadn't tagged the colonel with the name Fat Stick. He wasn't the most popular commander in the division; he used the swagger stick to magnify his gestures and give himself an imperious air. The only time he tucked it under his arm was when he was speaking to an officer of equal or superior rank, which struck me now as rather cowering, like a dog that tucks its tail between its legs. The more I thought about the destructive potential of the phrase the more I wished the chaplains hadn't thought of it. If it got around and Strand traced the origination back to them, I knew I'd be in serious trouble.

"Listen," I said, "if I were you I wouldn't say that, you know, about the stick anymore. That kind of talk is dangerous in this outfit."

"You mean blasphemous?" Duff asked.

"That's right," I said.

"It does have a ring to it, doesn't it?" Hallowell said and he smiled.

We started downhill and the organ bleated loudly. It didn't weigh much, something under fifty pounds, but it seemed to grow bulkier and heavier the longer we marched. Several men offered to lend us a hand, but Chaplain Duff refused. "We brought it and we'll carry it," he said.

The organ wheezed, jangled and moaned, and the sound carrying forward along the length of the column brought smiles and an occasional chuckle from the weary men. Sometimes a man would answer back with a prolonged and mournful "baaaa," like a lost sheep. This caught on and once while toiling up a rocky mountainside the whole company answered a groan from the organ with a rumbling "baaa, baaa."

I saw Colonel Pollard's figure limned against the hot sky. He stiffened. The swagger stick in his hand flashed angrily, then he turned and plunged down the ridge. It had become an endurance contest between the swagger stick and the organ. Pollard was determined to crush levity out of the men like juice out of grapes; he was determined to shake the organ out of the column.

The men, caught between swip-swop and B flat, buckled to it without complaint. They slogged through the heat. Perspiration soaking through their dungarees picked up the dust, so that after an hour they were running mud. There were no more baas from the men, but the organ continued to bleat and groan expressing the agony of the company and something of their grim determination not to give up to the stick.

It was grueling. It was swip-swop and baa every step of the way, but I could tell that the men were with the organ.

Occasionally Sergeant Strand dropped back and gave me a look that would have fried an egg and I knew he was hatching a special punishment for me, something worse than restriction, hanging, or disembowelment. His little eyes struck sparks and the tip of his cigar flashed red each time his eyes crossed mine, but evidently he believed Colonel Pollard would grind the chaplains down, because he didn't say anything. He'd watch us awhile, then he'd go forward to report our progress to the colonel at the head of the column.

We zigged, we zagged, we circled, but the chaplains

didn't tire; they marched along in the dust of the whole company, lugging all that religious paper and the organ. I thought the strain would get them bickering at one another, but there wasn't a bit of it. They had a cheery word for everybody and hiked along as if fifty miles was a stroll through the park.

Occasionally Chaplain Hallowell would pluck a flower from the trail side and examine it. "Interesting specimen," he would say, twirling the flower under his nose. "Unusual."

Then he'd take a folder out of his dungaree pocket and put the flower between the leaves. In twenty miles he had enough specimens to make a Caesar salad, including anchovies. That's right; we crossed the highway and hiked along the ocean front, scrambling through the tide flats, then inland again headed for the mountains.

It wasn't easy. It took heart, feet and muscle, but the chaplains carried on, and on, and on until dusk approached and the colonel had to stop. We hiked up one last sawback ridge, one final, nearly perpendicular obstacle, with the organ bleating all the way, then we linked up with A Company to establish a defense perimeter for the night.

When Strand dismissed the company, the men fell in their tracks with a sigh so close to B flat that Colonel Pollard's face turned bone white and he nearly amputated a trouser leg with his gnashing swagger stick.

All of us were numb from the waist down and from the neck up, but somewhere near the center of each man's heaving chest there was a sense of triumph because the chaplains and the organ had prevailed.

The company was strung out along a ridge so steep that

we had to dig shelves to prevent rolling down the hillside in our sleep. We hobbled about making camp. The night wind coming in off the ocean was cold, but we were ordered to keep our fires small and concealed below the rim of the hill. The colonel had it in his mind that we were in Korea and that a Chinese battalion was located on the next ridge over. We were so exhausted that we accepted this as a fact. Those who smoked lit only two cigarettes on a match. Everyone moved around in a constipated crouch so the enemy couldn't spot us against the skyline.

Down the line A Company—under Captain Crowell—had been in position since early afternoon. Some of them came over to have a look at us. They helped us gather wood and pitch shelter halves and showed themselves to be a helpful, happy lot of men in spite of the fact that they were fats.

A splinter moon came up revealing the European combat village a mile or so down the hill in front of us. It looked real in that pale light and A Company was going to defend it against our assault the following day. The fake town tended to discredit the presence of a Chinese battalion on the next hill so we relaxed a bit.

"Hell, they'd have had to cross Russia," one man said.

"I feel like I already did."

The chaplains and I were huddled around the weak blaze chafing our hands when I spotted Sergeant Major Strand's disembodied head caught in the firelight, and I knew the time of reckoning was at hand. He beckoned me. "Danbom!" he hissed.

I pushed myself up and followed him away from the fire. "What's the matter?" I asked.

One of Strand's afflictions was that he couldn't simply tell something. He had to act it out. Consequently if he wanted to say his right foot hurt he held up his right foot, pointed to it and groaned like a goaded steer. "My foot," he would say, pointing to his feet, "my right foot," he would add, touching his right foot to distinguish it from the left, "it hurts," he would conclude, grimacing to give definition to the word "hurts." Conversation of this nature kept Strand's limbs surprisingly supple for one of his age and frequently he was able to express rare ideas by a series of yoga-like contortions. He pointed at my head.

"You musta been behind the door when God passed out the brains!" he said.

"What is it, Sarge?" I asked.

"That box! That damned organ they're carrying."

"What about it?" I asked.

"It's fat! Get rid of it. It's driving the Old Man nuts!"

"The regulations state—"

"To hell with regulations," Strand growled. "It's fat. Get rid of it!"

I sighed. "Look, Sarge, Chaplain Duff mothers that organ."

"I don't give a damn what he mothers. The Old Man keeps expecting it to blow up or sprout wheels. Get rid of it!"

"The colonel has seen a field organ," I said.

"Not in any of his outfits, he hasn't. Not on a lean march like this, he hasn't. An organ? Get rid of it!"

"How?" I asked. "It's government property."

Strand bayoneted my chest with a horny finger. "So are you and I'm government. Roll it down the hill," he said and he jerked his head down the hill to demonstrate. "Drop it over a cliff." He dropped it over a cliff. "Hammer it to pieces." He hammered.

"Too noisy," I said.

"Bury it," Strand said and he dug with an imaginary intrenching tool.

"Ground's too hard up here."

Strand looked at me, his flinty eyes crackling. "It's your problem, Danbom, get me? Deep six that organ before morning or you can forget liberty for two weeks—among other things."

"Sarge!" I protested. "Our agreement didn't include organs."

"Tough. That's your problem." He moved off toward the C.P., clinging to the side of the hill like a massive goat.

I was torn by conflicting loyalties. My intent was to be a good Marine, to make a career in the Corps, but I'd shared the burden of the organ with the chaplains and along with the other men I couldn't help admiring their stamina. Still, I was a Marine first and a chaplain's assistant second and this only temporarily. I decided that my oath of allegiance to the United States Government and all duly constituted authority required me to get rid of the organ. After all, I'd sworn to support and defend the Constitution of the United States, not a portable field organ, however noble a symbol it may have become.

I crept back to the fire and shoved my chill hands toward its meager blaze. Chaplains Hallowell, Horowitz and

Duff had been joined by Sergeant Brody. Duff smiled at me cordially and I felt like Judas. I looked around for the organ, but couldn't locate it.

"Cold," I said. "Damp too. That organ ought to be under cover."

"Say, yes! Where is it?" Duff asked. He looked around. Chaplains Hallowell and Horowitz didn't know.

"Sergeant Brody," Duff asked, "is that field organ under cover? It shouldn't get damp."

"I'll take a look, sir," Brody said and he moved away into the darkness.

Duff thanked me. "Brody'll take care of it," he said.

"I'll just go along to help him."

Duff laid a restraining hand on my arm. "No need," he said quietly. "Enjoy the fire."

I think Duff sensed my intent because he gave me an awfully Christly smile, so knowing and forbearing that I felt truly murderous. Had the organ been in sight, I would have thrown myself upon it and hacked it to bits.

I waited until I thought I could slip away, but before I could manage it Brody reappeared. He looked around worriedly, then cupped his hands to his mouth and in his fine, rolling baritone voice yelled along the ridge: "Hey! Any you guys seen Chaplain Duff's organ?"

The wind picked up these words and boomed them down the company line. They echoed through the ravines. "Duff's organ, organ, organ."

There was a significant silence.

"Any you guys seen Chaplain Duff's organ?" Brody hollered again and he started toward A Company.

Duff sat on his haunches frowning into the fire, then a

peculiar expression crossed his face. He scrambled to his feet and went after Brody.

"Has he lost it?" someone from A Company yelled.

"He shoulda tied a string on it!" came from B Company further along the ridge.

Duff caught Brody's arm. "Field organ," he whispered urgently. "Portable field organ!"

"How big is it?" someone called.

"About three feet," Brody responded.

"Wahoo! Hoo. Hoo!"

The whole battalion let out a whoop of laughter which reverberated through the hills. Weary men came to life and howled.

"Field organ," Chaplain Duff hollered.

All down the line men turned out to search for Duff's organ. The wit wasn't choice, but it drew waves of laughter. Squads beat the brush trying to find the missing organ.

The ridge rocked with pithy sayings.

"Did you say it was portable, Padre?" someone called out of the darkness.

"Field organ," Duff kept yelling. "Field organ!"

"It'll turn up, Padre."

Howls!

Chaplain Duff had enough. "All right, all right, you wise guys!" he roared. "Bring me the first organ you find with keys and foot pedals that can play the Marine Hymn!" He returned to the fire and sat down in brooding silence.

I saw Strand running, scrambling, sliding toward me along the stony hillside and knew that I'd never see Ella again. Strand was frenzied. He slipped in the loose shale and started down the mountainside, but pawed his way back. At first he was too choked with fury to speak coherently. "*Aaragh!*" he rumbled, flailing his arms.

"Strand!" I said.

He lashed out at me with a bear swipe of his big arm. I ducked and the momentum of his blow nearly catapulted him down the hill.

"Sarge," I said. "I tried."

"Organist!" he rumbled. "Traitor! Security broken. Position revealed. Danbom, you die!"

He lunged at me, his great hands lusting for my windpipe. I threw myself to the ground and Strand plunged over me headlong down the hill. I heard him thrashing through the sparse scrub like a drunken rhinoceros. Boulders rolled and loose shale he dislodged built into a landslide. Strand fought for traction, his hands and feet working like tank treads, the breath rumbling in his throat, but he couldn't stop until he hit the bottom where he coursed about rutting and uprooting like a primordial beast in the pit of hell.

I'd reached the end of my tether. Strand's attack meant total war. I searched for the most defiant phrase I could think of and hurled it down on him.

"Fat stick!" I yelled. "Strand, there's no difference between that fat stick and an organ except that one plays music!"

Black silence. The quarter-moon died in the night sky. Strand stood below me, petrified. The fatal words were whispered along the ridge and I knew that I'd struck a blow against the order of the universe.

Terrified, I moved my sleeping bag away from the others to a secluded niche where I sat rocking back and forth in woe, anguish and loneliness. The moon reappeared and far off over the hills I could see the ocean pressed like a silver knife against the dark sky. I was cut off from my fellow man once more. I had raised up the Girl from Escondido to win my place among them, but I knew she couldn't protect me from the effects of the blasphemous phrase "fat stick." I cursed the chaplains for having invented it. I cursed myself for having uttered it.

I was a virgin orphan pariah. A Jonah. And I understood at last the madness and the misery of Job.

The night was thick with whispers and all about me were ghosts and phantoms and fears. I saw cardboard faces on the moon, my mother, my father, the Girl from Escondido in a stewardess' cap. Interdom. I was plagued by begats and by Brother Queen's voice:

> "Now of that long pursuit
> Comes on at hand the bruit;
> That voice is round me like a bursting sea."

I groaned. My earth indeed was marred and shattered in shard on shard. Hounds of heaven!

I thought of Ella, the one anchor and only hope in my drifting life. "Ella," I said aloud, "save me."

In the morning, I crept out warily. Chaplain Duff's organ had been found, neatly wrapped in a poncho to prevent its getting damp. No one seemed to care whether or not I was alive or dead and their lack of concern increased my unease.

While the company officers heard a lecture on discipline

and security which Colonel Pollard punctuated with pistol-like reports of his sacred swagger stick, Sergeant Brody took the chaplains aside to instruct them in the use of the field compass.

It was a warm morning with an innocent blue sky and I was packing my gear when I noticed Max Laperuta passing out Bibles to the men. This was such an uncharacteristic thing for Laperuta to be doing that I felt a premonitory apprehension. I looked around and saw Weller thumbing clumsily through one of the Bibles while Powell and Morgan hung over his shoulders.

"Between Ecclesiastes and Isaiah," Powell said.

"Who are they?" Weller asked.

Powell snatched the Bible from Weller and turned through it. "Here," he said. "The Song of Solomon."

They began to read, scrambling over each other to get at the words.

I stood paralyzed while all about me men read the Song of Solomon, exclaiming now and then as a phrase I had applied to the Girl from Escondido caught their attention.

"It's her!" Weller cried. "They wrote her up."

"Stupid," Powell declared, "he made her up."

"Why, she's right here in the book," Weller said truculently. "See here: 'Thy navel is like a round goblet . . .' "

"Yeah, but she ain't black, but comely, stupid," Morgan said.

I knew retribution would be swift, but I hadn't expected it to take this form. Obviously the chaplains had distributed their wares and those Bibles like the stones used to crush life out of the ancient martyrs were flattening the Girl from Escondido.

Colonel Pollard appeared, walking along the ridge with Strand at his side. Seeing his men poring so intently over the books the colonel halted and turned to Strand. "What are these men doing, Sergeant?" he demanded.

Strand looked around carefully. He saw several of the men moving their lips and tracing the words with their fingertips. His face brightened. "They're reading, sir," he said.

The swagger stick cut a permanent slash in the air and impacted on the colonel's calf. "I know they're reading, man! *What* are they reading?"

Strand snatched a Bible from the nearest group and examined it. He looked at the cover and turned to the title page. "The Holy Bible, sir," he said.

Colonel Pollard exhaled and seemed to diminish in size. He drew a breath that rustled the leaves of the Bible in Strand's paw and fixed the sergeant with an icy glare. "Suppose we stow the Bibles and pass the ammunition, Sergeant," he said.

"Yes, sir!" Strand replied smartly.

"A Company has gone into position and we're due to attack them if you'll remember."

"I do, sir," Strand said.

"Then let's get on with it!"

The colonel vanished, leaving Strand with his saluting arm half cocked.

I ran down the hill and found the Chaplains with Sergeant Brody. They each had a compass in hand.

"Now, gentlemen," Brody was saying, "we know enough about the compass and map to start using them in a practical way. If each of you will take your compass and align the front sight hairline on that tree over there we'll locate our present position on the map."

Brody pointed to a eucalyptus tree a hundred yards away. It was the only tree of its size in the area. "That tree, gentlemen, the eucalyptus. Sight on that tree and each of you read your azimuth to me."

The chaplains aimed their compasses at the eucalyptus tree.

"What is your reading?" Brody asked.

"One hundred twenty-two degrees," Hallowell said.

"Two hundred seventy-eight degrees," Horowitz said.

"Fifty-one degrees," Duff said.

Brody glanced at the eucalyptus tree. He frowned.

"Curious," he said. He pointed once more to the eucalyptus tree. "You all sighting on the same tree?"

The chaplains looked at the eucalyptus tree. They nodded.

To show that he'd grasped the principle at least, Hallowell suggested maybe they ought to stand closer together.

"If you was standing inside each other it wouldn't help!" Brody said. "Let's try again, shall we?"

This time Brody sighted on the tree himself. His reading was sixty degrees off north.

"All right, gentlemen," he said. "How do you read it this time?"

The chaplains gave the same readings they had given before. One hundred twenty-two degrees. Two hundred seventy-eight degrees. Fifty-one degrees.

Brody's ruddy face turned half a shade darker. "Why, it looks like the North Pole has taken a vacation," he said. "Looks like the Old North Pole decided to take a stroll down toward the equator, or maybe I just caught that eucalyptus when it stopped running. My reading was sixty degrees."

The chaplains stared at their compasses.

Chaplain Horowitz frowned. "There's only one north," he said.

"No, there's magnetic north and true north," Chaplain Duff said.

"You have to adjust for it, Nathan," Chaplain Hallowell said.

"Let Duff adjust," Horowitz exclaimed irritably. "He adjusts as the wind listeth, but my north is true."

"Nathan," Hallowell said gently, "we can't all have been looking at the true tree."

Brody was dumbfounded. His compass hung in his hand.

"I am looking at the true tree!" Horowitz cried. "Duff is the one given to visions."

"There's only one eucalyptus," Duff cried.

"There's millions of eucalyptuses," Horowitz said.

"Eucalypti!"

"I most certainly did not. Eucalypt yourself."

"Gentlemen," Brody hollered. "Chaplains, let me see your compasses."

The chaplains held out their compasses and Brody looked at them. "Ah," he said, "let's go back to our first lesson in the use of the compass. The first thing you do when you take a reading is to push the little catch which releases the compass needle." Brody shook his head. "You can't find north with your needles locked," he said.

The chaplains regarded Brody attentively.

"The sergeant speaks in parables," Chaplain Horowitz said presently.

The chaplains pushed the release on their compasses and watched the needles swing.

"North," they said.

"Now what reading do you get on that tree?" Brody asked.

"Sixty degrees," they said.

Brody glanced at me. "They're really semper fidelis," he said. Then he went up the hill to get ready for our push on the European combat town.

As the chaplains packed their gear I noticed they distributed the load equally. All of the Bibles were gone, so Horowitz carried New Testaments and Hallowell carried Catholic missals.

Duff packed the menorah.

Being a chaplain's assistant I assumed that I'd earned the status of a noncombatant, but as the chaplains and I started down the hill toward the aid station which was located on the far side of the combat town Strand hailed me. "Danbom! Where you think you're going?"

"Battalion Aid Station," I said. "I'm a noncombatant."

"Not in this outfit you ain't. You're in the first assault section; now haul ass up here and draw your ammunition."

I handed my end of the organ to Duff, who suggested I might appeal to the Geneva Convention, but I pointed out that Geneva was a long way off and Strand was only twenty feet away. The chaplains wished me luck.

I was too deeply engaged in my own problems to take

much interest in making a mock assault on a mock town, but as I fell in line to get my issue of blank cartridges I noticed Laperuta and Morgan grinning at me tigerishly.

When I reached the armorer who was passing out the blanks, he closed the ammo box. "Fresh out, Danbom," he said.

I looked around at the men still in line behind me. "Come on," I said. "What about these guys?"

The armorer was a lean, freckle-faced corporal with a wise-guy grin and gum in his mouth. "They're goin' to share with you, Danbom," he said. "Yeah, I got a hunch that's what they'll do."

"Come on, I can't fight without ammo."

"Most of these are just blanks anyway, Danbom," the armorer said.

"What do you mean 'most'?"

The freckles on the armorer's face blended into a dark mass as his grin broadened. "Oh, we get careless now and then," he said. "Sometimes we slip a real one in by mistake. You know how it is, Danbom. Like maybe some guys'll slip a fake one in for real?"

The men around me chuckled deep in their throats like lions at feeding time.

"Come on in there, let's hustle," Strand bellowed.

The man behind prodded me roughly with his rifle butt.

"Come on, Danbom," Laperuta called. "We got a demonstration over here."

I went to where the company had gathered around Sergeant Strand. Glancing back I saw the armorer passing out more clips and I thought fleetingly of the chaplains' argument about the transubstantiation of bullets. I wondered if they could turn real when they hit the target, because there was no doubt in my mind that I was it.

Strand waited for the last man, then he put a canteen cup on the end of an M1 rifle and held it up. "Now, men," he said, "these here blanks are dangerous and we wouldn't want anyone to get hurt, would we?"

He looked at me and grinned around the dead cigar in his face.

"No," several men said.

"These things pack a lot of muzzle velocity," Strand continued. "They can burn like hell and the wads raise a welt the size of an egg if you hit a man at twenty feet. Get that? Twenty feet."

"Right," several men said.

Strand pulled the trigger and the explosion sent the canteen cup sailing sixty feet into the air.

The men watched it go up and watched it come down. When it hit the ground all eyes were resting on me.

"Hot as a blow torch," Strand said. "All right, let's go."

I was wringing wet. They were going to kill me with fake bullets in a mock assault on a phony town because the Girl from Escondido wasn't real.

And who would protest? Not my mother, or my father, not Ella, not anyone in the world. And the chaplains would bury me and get some actual experience in graves registration. They alone would benefit by my demise.

I'd often wondered what doomed men thought about and found it was nothing more than the dumb hope for deliverance, the dumb, benumbing hope that his last few moments are a dream from which he will awaken.

We divided into fire teams and started down toward the combat town.

Strand had assigned me to a team with Laperuta, Powell, Weller and Morgan. Laperuta pulled a Bible from his blouse pocket and thrust it at me. "You're going to need this, Danbom, you creep," he said.

"It didn't say anything in there about her coming from Escondido," Weller said.

"Will you wise up, Weller!" Powell exclaimed. "There is no Girl from Escondido!"

"What about the bite on his shoulder?" Weller asked. "What about that?"

Morgan groaned. "Weller," he said, "Strand saw Danbom bite himself."

"Did you bite yourself, Danbom?" Weller asked.

We were advancing across a field waiting for the signal to attack. "Boys," I said nervously, "there's been a misunderstanding. I told you she went to New Mexico for her lungs, Weller."

"You're going to need a new set too," Laperuta said. "He made suckers of us all, didn't he, boys? He don't have a girl; he never had a girl. He just plain lied out of the Bible."

"I've got a girl," I said.

"Sure," Laperuta said with heavy irony, "her hair is as a flock of goats. Some pig you got!"

"Listen! I got a real girl!"

"You want to swear on a stack of Bibles, Danbom?" Morgan asked. "We got 'em."

At that moment the whistle blew and the men on both flanks ran toward me. I heard a report and a shaft of flame boosted me into a frantic dash toward the combat town. I ran like a rabbit with the whole platoon strung out behind me firing blanks at my tail and howling vengeance.

I skittered into the street, cut down an alleyway and was met by a hail of fire from every door and window.

Colored-smoke grenades were lobbed from the rooftops, filling the streets with red, yellow and green smoke. I dove through the window of a hofbrau and met Strand, who fired a clip at me from his forty-five. I dove out another window into a cloud of sulphurous smoke, rolled to my feet and ran straight into a machine gun which burned my right dungaree leg off.

I reeled away, choking, half blind. Hands reached through a haze of red smoke, hoisted me up and threw me down on my back. When my eyes cleared, Laperuta was seated on my chest. We were inside a simulated church. Outside, the mock battle continued, but most of the H and S Company men were looking down at me from vantage points on the scaffolding which supported the plaster walls.

Powell had my right arm, Morgan had my left and Weller held my feet.

"All right, Danbom," Laperuta said. "Let's have it. What are you?"

"An orphan?" I said hopefully.

"Yeah, what else? Let's hear it."

Morgan twisted my arm and Weller reversed the natural position of my left foot.

"A liar!" I yelled manfully.

Weller groaned. "But Danbom, she's in the book!"

"Weller, will you get with it?" Morgan declared. "That book is a couple of hundred years old."

"Yeah, but I got a lock of her hair! What about that?"

Laperuta sat harder on my chest and took a handful of my singed hair. "We know you're a liar, Danbom," he said. "We know that. But what else are you? Tell the boys."

I squirmed like a weasel. "Chaplain's assistant."

"Work on him a little, boys," Laperuta said. "We know you're a chaplain's assistant, Charlie boy. But what else?"

Powell, Weller and Morgan were tying me in knots. "A lying, orphan, chaplain's assistant!" I screeched. "And I bit myself!"

"Come on, Danbom!" Laperuta said and he bounced on my rib cage. "It begins with 'V,' like Virginia."

"Listen, I can explain," I countered.

"Say it, Danbom."

I bit my tongue. They racked my limbs. I thought of Ella, wondering if she could love a permanent cripple. I remembered Benny Cohen who, under less painful but similarly compelling circumstances, had falsely professed to believe in Tinker Bell. They were killing me. "All right!" I cried. "Virgin!"

"Who's a virgin?" Laperuta demanded.

"I'm a virgin!" I shrieked.

They dropped me. Powell, Weller and Morgan backed away as though I carried the plague.

Weller was particularly stricken, so much so that even in my agony my heart went out to him. He stared down at me, shaking his head dumbly from side to side. "But my hair," he said. "What about my pretty lock of hair?"

"Weller," I said, "I got it off a dog."

"She's not a dog!" Weller retorted. "She's beautiful!"

"No, Weller, a real dog."

It took Weller a moment. Then a cry of despair broke from his lips. "Oh!" he wailed, "I been worshiping the hair of a dog instead of the girl who bit him!"

He fell upon me with the fury of one whose faith has been betrayed and would have gouged out my eyes if Morgan and Powell hadn't pulled him off.

Laperuta grinned down into my face and patted my cheek. "Danbom, you're a lying, mother-loving, orphan, virgin, chaplain's assistant," he said. "You're some Marine!" He got off my chest and stood up with a triumphant leer on his face. "Some Marine," he repeated.

There was a lull in the firing as the men in the building stared at me, their former idol brought so low. I was crushed, but I mustered one last measure of defiance. Struggling to my feet I faced them all. "I'm not the only one!" I yelled. "There are others. Other liars and other virgins too! Right here! If you had any guts you'd admit it."

To a man they turned their rifles on me and spat fire. I ran. I reached the street and slammed into Colonel Pollard standing in a patch of green smoke and berating his officers for the chaos of our attack. I ducked away and scuttled toward the sound of the organ.

When the chaplains saw me running toward the aid station they jumped up, aghast.

"He's all shot to hell!" Horowitz exclaimed.

Duff caught me as I staggered to my knees. "What happened, son?" he asked.

"It was the Bibles, sir," I gasped. "They got me."

Seven

HAVING been stripped of pride and honor and any hope of advancement in my chosen career, I saw no harm in confiding in the chaplains. They were the only ones who would listen; the men laughed at the sight of me.

The chaplains were both contrite and confused. They apologized for having told Laperuta about the Song of Solomon. He'd come to them, his Machiavellian blood still boiling over my preeminence in the ladies' department, to warn them of my moral turpitude.

"He said you had this broad," Hallowell said, "the term was his, not mine. But I recognized the quotation at once."

"Yes," Duff said, "the minute he said her belly was like a heap of wheat we knew. He seemed quite surprised."

"Take a look at a heap of wheat sometime," Horowitz said. "A loaf of bread, maybe, but a heap of wheat is nonsense."

I told them why I'd invented a girl from Escondido and pretended to have illicit relations with her.

They agreed that lying about illicit relations was sinful.

Chaplain Duff declared that there was little to choose between carnal thoughts and carnal deeds.

Common sense told me this wasn't so, but to avoid alienating my last contact with humanity I nodded my head, lying again.

Duff thought I should do the right thing by the girl.

"What girl?" I asked.

"Ella Budd," he said.

"But I hardly know her."

"That's the other one," Horowitz said.

"The figment of his imagination," Hallowell said.

"Some figment," Horowitz said. "Wheat, grapes, pomegranates and honeycomb. He could do better in a health food store."

"Of course, you can't marry her if she doesn't exist," Duff said.

"Even if her uncle would let me," I said.

They were confused and I wasn't so sure myself. I began to wonder if maybe Ella wasn't also a figment of my imagination.

"When you get back to camp, why don't you call her?" Duff suggested.

"What if she doesn't answer?"

"Have faith," Hallowell said. "Faith is the substance of things hoped for, the evidence of things not seen."

"Haven't you ever had that feeling?" I asked. "Like maybe there's no one at the other end of the line?"

They glanced at each other.

"Our problem, Danbom," Horowitz said, "is that on one connection we're likely to get three different answers."

"I've noticed," I said.

Chaplain Duff sighed. "Well, one thing is obvious, Danbom. You can't have two girls in one person."

"Why, Father Duff," Horowitz declared, "I thought you believed in the Holy Trinity. In your God there are three divine persons: the Father, Son and Holy Ghost."

"That's an entirely different matter," Duff said testily. "Either Danbom has a girl, or he hasn't."

"Or he has two," Horowitz said.

"Or one and a figment," Hallowell said.

I began to wish I hadn't taken them into my confidence.

Through the haze left by the smoke grenades I saw the combat village standing like a movie set for an old guts and glory action picture. The last fire teams were coming through, running and dodging, playing out the drama they'd often seen on the silver screen. The men who were too tired to play anymore clutched their bellies and pitched forward, or grabbed their throats and fell to the ground with cries of strangulated agony.

Colonel Pollard appeared out of the smoke and watched his men, pleased by the improvement in their performance. "That's go!" he shouted as Morgan flopped and writhed, refusing to die. "That's go!"

Morgan rose again and fired into the smoke, staggering under the impact of a thousand rounds of pretend bullets. "Oh, that's go!" Pollard raved and Morgan dropped forward on his face spread-eagled in a cruciform and I began to see that it wasn't how one lived, but how one died that caught the colonel's eye.

After Morgan's star performance, sure to win him another stripe, the colonel passed the order to secure and vanished in a cloud of yellow smoke.

I changed my dungarees, discarding the charred pair I had been wearing, and smeared my face with salve to take the sting out of the flash burns. The sun was going down and I welcomed the coolness. The chaplains drifted off to eat, but I wasn't hungry so I lay back and closed my eyes.

I must have dozed off because Sergeant Strand's voice brought me around. He was talking to a cluster of noncoms, his heavy cheekbones rosy with indignation. He held up five fingers. "Five hands he blitzed me. Five! I deal and win one hand and pick up another to blitz Brody with when along comes this Padre Horowitz and gives Brody a signal."

"A signal?" Laperuta asked.

"A signal," Strand says and he nods. "I say to Brody let's go another hand, ready to blitz hell out of him, but that kibitzer Horowitz comes with a signal."

"What signal?"

"'*Goot shaabas,*'" Strand said. "'With you, Brody, there is a *minyan,*' he says, and with that Brody throws down the cards. Says he can't play no more. Goot shaabas. They were in cahoots. What's wrong, I say. The Sabbath, Brody says. Get that!"

I got up and walked over to where they were standing. "That's right," I said.

Strand turned on me. "Don't start with me, Virgin," he said, which drew a laugh. "I know the difference."

"Strand," I declared, "you're stupid. Has it ever occurred to you that you're stupid?"

Strand slewed his big head from side to side in disbelief. "Stupid?" he said. "I'm stupid?"

"For the Jews the Sabbath begins on Friday when the sun goes down and ends Saturday night. Horowitz is holding services for the men of Hebrew faith."

"For Brody? If he's Jewish so am I!"

"Go then!" I cried. "You've got the vocabulary. Kibitzer, blitz . . ."

"That's not Jewish, that's gin," Strand declared.

"Strand," I said, "you're so stupid you don't know gin from Jewish." I saw a kind of crazed expression on Strand's face which frequently appeared on Hallowell's when he conducted the choir. His throat constricted, his eyes rolled and he reached toward me with both hands, but before he could make contact the colonel passed the order to fall in for the march back to camp.

Strand fixed me with a baleful glare and shook his head. "Danbom," he said, "Danbom, I've lit a lot of cigars in this man's outfit, but I have never seen a crummier, creepier, cruddier, foul-up than you are. I wash my hands of you. We all wash our hands of you."

The non-coms nodded. Laperuta looked right through me. They all looked right through me and I got the terrible feeling I wasn't there.

Strand bawled for the company to fall in and ten minutes later we were marching back to camp.

I had expected derision, laughter and catcalling, but not one man in that outfit met my eyes. They looked around me, over me and through me with such marvelously simulated indifference that if the chaplains hadn't acknowledged my presence I would have sworn I was something I had made up, like my mother and my father.

All that long march back my very existence depended on those chaplains. They spoke to me and I answered them. They wanted to know how I was.

"I'm not sure I am," I said.

"You're not sure you are what?" Horowitz asked.

"Anything," I said.

They took me seriously. If they hadn't I would have vanished and never been heard of again.

I'd heard of Coventry, of the silent treatment; it was a cruel weapon we were not above using against our orphan fellows at Interdom. We'd used it on Benny Cohen and driven him away, but I'd never experienced it myself. And I began to see that the evidence of one's existence is more or less statistical. Out of approximately three hundred men in the company only three recognized me—the chaplains—and their recognition was somewhat disconcerting because they each saw me in a different light. But at best I was only 3/300ths there.

The crowning blow was delivered by Weller at Las Pulgas. We arrived at camp dog-tired and when the formation broke I staggered straight into Weller, nearly knocking him down. Our faces were not four inches apart, but he looked beyond me with a truly puzzled and angry expression. "Who threw that!" he yelled.

He didn't see me! He really didn't.

"Weller," I said, "it's me, Danbom!"

He stepped past me. "Damn you, Morgan," he yelled. "I saw you throw that!" And he chased Morgan into their hut and commenced to tussle with him.

When I reached our hut I lay down and pulled a blanket over my head. I was afraid to call Ella. I was not only afraid she wouldn't be there to answer, but that if she answered I wouldn't be there to hear.

The chaplains were considerate. They left me alone, but they referred to me frequently in their conversation, enough times so that I was finally able to fall asleep with some assurance that I would, indeed, wake up.

Saturday was a half day for the troops. There was an inspection in the morning, so we cleaned up after our two days in the field. Chaplain Duff field-stripped his field organ, dusted it out and oiled the hinges with Three-in-One oil. I stumbled through the morning routine half hoping for a breach in the barrier of silence which had been imposed against me. There was none. At chow no one spoke to me. During inspection the colonel passed me by without a glance and Strand ordered the men to "close up ranks in there," just as though the space in which I was standing was vacant.

After inspection I went back to my bunk and lay down feeling like a mummy.

The Fats and Go chorus had grown to thirty members and that afternoon they drifted into the hut to rehearse for their debut the following morning. As a general rule the choristers were more tolerant than the other men and I was grateful when a couple of them sniggered in my direction. It gave me enough hope to contemplate committing suicide. I lay there actually enjoying the prospect and running through ways of doing it. Hanging seemed to be the best. My limp body suspended on the end of a noose drew enough self-pity so that I nearly wept for poor Danbom. But being an orphan takes the steam out of suicide as a protest. There was no one close enough to really care, except me. I abandoned the notion, but it had had a certain palliative effect. I decided there was a distinction between being an unacknowledged, orphan, virgin Marine and being dead, but not much.

I rolled over and watched the chorus at the other end of the hut. Chaplain Duff was accompanying them on the organ while Hallowell put them through their paces. He ran a taut chorus, rapping the music stand insistently with his baton for attention. There was no fooling around, no talking, no boondoggling, and the choristers took him seriously.

They were singing old 124th, "Turn Back O Man," repeating certain phrases over and over again until Hallowell was completely satisfied. I watched him with growing fascination. I'd never closely observed the contortions of a conductor's face. Hallowell mouthed the words, throwing back his head to reach for a tenor passage, then tucking his chin down into his collarbone to dive for the bass notes. One eye cocked a warning at the baritones, the other swung on the tenor section while he mouthed the labial shapes he wanted. It was more than the human face was built to withstand and through it all there was an idiotic expression of musical ecstasy and the baton kept slashing cubes of time out of the air.

At the end of two hours I began to understand how Hallowell, thin as he looked, was capable of thirty push-ups. Anyone who can bend, twist, sway, and keep his arms chopping and weaving in the air for two solid hours has got to be made of spring steel.

When the choir members left, Chaplain Horowitz appeared. His religious observances were over and his face was stormy. He crossed to his locker, pulled out a fresh shirt and began to put it on, grumbling ominously to himself. Hallowell and Duff watched him for a time, then asked where he was going.

"To the dance at the Officers' Club," Horowitz responded irritably.

"To a dance!" Hallowell exclaimed. "You just hiked a hundred miles. What do you want to go dancing for?"

"Because I wasn't invited," Horowitz replied.

Duff nodded agreeably as though not being invited to a dance was the best possible reason for going.

"Were you invited?" Horowitz asked Hallowell.

"No," Hallowell said.

"Then you were excluded," Horowitz said flatly.

"Come on, Nathan," Duff said. "Why excluded?"

"Because we're chaplains, for one thing," Horowitz said furiously. "Hath not a chaplain eyes? Hath not a chaplain hands, organs, dimensions, senses, affections, passions . . ."

"An organ we have," Hallowell said.

"If you prick us, do we not bleed? If you tickle us, do we not laugh? If you poison us, do we not die?"

Hallowell and Duff watched Horowitz button his uniform blouse. He was going to the dance if his legs dropped off.

"Do you like to dance?" Hallowell asked.

"I don't dance," Horowitz grumbled.

"Then why in hell are you going!" Hallowell cried.

"Because it's restricted!" Horowitz declared.

Hallowell moaned, went to his locker and took his uniform out. "All right," he said, "I'll go with you."

Chaplain Duff shrugged and began to dress.

They went to the dance.

I tossed about on my bunk, considering my shattered prospects. I was too weary to sleep, too heartsick to think of calling Ella. As long as I was in the Marine Corps I knew the story of my shame would follow me. Far off there was the sound of merriment; the word about me was going around like a breeze in dead grass. My bawd from Escondido had bitten deep and left a wound from which I would never recover.

I writhed.

I dozed and dreamed I was dancing with Ella, turning round, round and around, waltzing; but it was a cardboard face with a manikin grin and across her belly, like a heap of wheat set about with lilies, was a sign which read FLY NOW, PAY LATER.

I had paid. My face burned; my legs ached. I was sorely tried. The Girl from Escondido came into my dreams more real to me now than Ella would ever be.

I pitched and tossed. I vowed once more to never, under any circumstances, pretend. I vowed to forsake all false and imaginary things. No more books. No more guts and glory action films. No more dreams. I rededicated myself to hard and substantial reality supported by evidence of the common senses. Seeing, touching, tasting, smelling and hearing was now, and forever more, believing.

I fell into a fitful slumber and much later was awakened

by the sound of the chaplains' voices. I turned back my blanket and saw them at their end of the hut. The beam of a flashlight projected their shadows upward on the ribs of our Quonset hut as they got ready for bed.

"Brandy," Hallowell said.

"Why Brandy?" Horowitz asked.

"Her name is Brandy because she was born in Wilmington, Delaware," Hallowell said. "Her full first name is Brandywine."

"Doubly intoxicating," Duff said.

"From the bedroom window of the hospital her mother could see the Brandywine River where it joins the Delaware. Her parents flipped a coin. It came up Brandywine, otherwise she would have been called Dela, short for Delaware."

"Good thing she wasn't born in Providence," Duff said. "It might have come up Pawtuxet. How'd you like a girl called Paw?"

"She's not my girl. All I did was dance with her," Hallowell said.

"Four times."

Horowitz pulled his flannel nightgown over his head; his great shadow on the ceiling flapped its wings like a huge bat. "You learned a lot about this girl," he said.

"In four dances you learn a lot."

"Who is she?" Duff asked.

"Colonel Pollard's daughter," Hallowell said.

I saw Horowitz' batlike shadow freeze. Then he struggled to pull his head through his nightshirt. "Colonel Pollard's daughter?" he hissed. "Colonel Pollard's daughter!"

"She's lovely," Duff said.

"Don't listen to him," Horowitz exclaimed. "He's a *shadchan* in sheep's clothing! Colonel Pollard's daughter! You were dancing with her and you knew it?"

"It's a free country, Nathan," Duff said.

"Free?" Horowitz cried. "Maybe the rest is free but I tell you chaplains in the Marine Corps are in bondage." Horowitz flailed his arms and fell on his bunk.

"She's home from school. She graduated," Hallowell said.

"Tell her to go back, post graduate. We'll take a collection!"

"I only danced with her," Hallowell said.

"Danced!" Horowitz cried. "Snuggled, cooed, twisted, watusied."

"That's an exaggeration."

"Did I hear Captain Crowell complain chaplains are not supposed to have sex appeal? Did I?"

"Did you?" Hallowell asked.

"With my own ears!" Horowitz said. "Right here on my head. Colonel Pollard will roast us like Shadrach, Meshach and Abednego."

"She's interested in choir music. She's coming tomorrow to hear us," Hallowell said.

"So is Miss Budd," Duff said.

I sat bolt up. Duff saw me and came to my bunk. "Ella?" I croaked.

Duff nodded, smiling. "I called her," he said. "Hope you don't mind, but my curiosity got the better of me."

"She's coming, tomorrow, to chapel?"

"Yes. She seemed quite delighted to learn that there were

three chaplains here and that you were, in fact, our assistant."

"She asked about me?"

"Yes, she did."

"Chaplain Duff," I said, "you've made me the happiest man in the world."

"The three of us would like to talk to the three of you after the service," Duff said.

"Three of who?" I asked.

"Her uncle, Chief Budd, is coming too."

"Oh," I said. "Well, I guess that's all right."

"He's her guardian, you know."

"No, I didn't."

Duff smiled and shook his head. "There seem to be a lot of tangled relationships in this situation, Danbom. I think we ought to get to the bottom of it, don't you?"

"Yes, sir. I'd sure like to get it straightened out."

Duff frowned slightly. "She *is* the only girl you have, isn't she?"

"Yes, sir, she is."

"Hmmmm," he said.

"Chaplain Duff?"

"Yes?"

"You're talking to me, right?"

"I am," he said.

Chaplains Hallowell and Horowitz came and stood with Duff at the foot of my bunk.

"Do you know the bit about the tree?" I asked.

"What tree?" Horowitz asked.

"I think I heard it at Interdom; you know, about the tree in the forest that no one sees, that falls and no one hears? Like you take that eucalyptus you were aiming your compasses at yesterday. Are you sure it's still there?"

Duff nodded. "Berkeleyan idealism," he said.

"That's it," Hallowell said. "*Esse est percipi.* To be is to be perceived. The tree is still there, Danbom."

"Are you sure?"

"I'll go out and have a look," Horowitz said.

"Yeah, but when you aren't looking, what then?" I asked. "I know it's stupid, but it's an idea that bugs hell out of orphans. You know, the idea that maybe it goes away."

"Danbom," Hallowell said, "the good Lord is watching all the trees. We know the men are giving you the silent treatment, but you're perceived, so go to sleep."

"I'll keep an eye on you if you like," Horowitz said. "And in the morning we'll both go over and have a look. After all, a tree is a tree, but two girls in one, there's a different thing."

They went to bed and the last thing I remember as I dozed off was that Horowitz was watching me.

In the morning Chaplain Hallowell combed his hair several times and Horowitz watched him suspiciously. "If you don't look out you'll have a *shviger* who carries a swagger stick."

"What?" Hallowell exclaimed, his comb poised in mid-air.

"He means your mother-in-law might carry a fat stick like the Old Man," Duff said.

Horowitz looked at Duff, surprised. "*Dominus vobiscum,*" he said.

After chow I did my best to minimize the facial cuts, burns, bruises and abrasions left by my encounter with the boys in combat town. Every muscle in my body was sore and the bite on my shoulder had turned black. Hallowell's choir drifted in for one last rehearsal and I wandered over to the chapel to wait for Ella and the chief.

Our chapel was a white building with peaked windows and a steeple, located on a rise of ground between the H.Q. building and the main camp. It had lawn around it, and a couple of cottonwood trees laid welcome shadows across the paths. I sat down on the front stoop to watch Basilone Road for Chief Budd's pickup truck. It was too soon to expect Ella and the chief, but I hoped maybe she'd come early so we could have a few minutes together before the service began.

The longer I waited the more I worried she wouldn't come. I thought about calling to check, but weighing the disappointment if she couldn't come against the suspense of waiting, I decided not to call.

I went inside to see if there were hymnals in all the pews. There were. Presently Chaplains Hallowell, Horowitz and Duff arrived with the choir. Duff gave me the order of service to distribute at the door. The text on the cover was from Ecclesiastes: "Wisdom is better than weapons of war; but one sinner destroyeth much good."

When I'd read it I glanced at Duff, who smiled. "Hallowell selected it," he said.

"I'm the sinner, is that it?" I asked.

"You're not the only one. The three of us have been doing our share. Not meshing. We talked it over last night. We're going to try to be less fat. A couple of officers took us aside at the dance and clued us in on Colonel Pollard's problems. It's not easy to put an outfit like this in shape."

"No, sir," I said. "It's not easy."

"Captain Crowell of A Company was particularly helpful."

I nodded. Crowell's motive was obvious. When the colonel had anyone in H and S Company he didn't like he usually transferred him to Crowell who was, no doubt, afraid he'd get stuck with the chaplains if they didn't toe the mark. "That was nice of him," I said.

Duff took my arm and lowered his voice. "Crowell is engaged to Miss Pollard," he said.

"Is that right?"

"Yes, poor Hallowell was quite distraught when he heard it." Duff glanced at Hallowell and shook his head sympathetically. "It's difficult, isn't it?" he said. "Well, when Miss Budd comes, be sure I meet her. She seemed very pleasant on the phone. She didn't ask about your other girl, but I do think, to be fair, Charles, that you should make up your mind."

I started to explain once more, but I saw that Duff was fixed on the notion that every romantic relationship was by nature triangular. Hallowell, Miss Pollard, Captain Crowell. Me, Ella and the Girl from Escondido. He was unable to abandon his trinitarian mode of thinking.

People were beginning to come in so I went to the door to pass out the orders of service.

Colonel Pollard arrived with his daughter and Captain Crowell. He took an order of service from me, glanced at it and turned to Crowell. "What in hell is All Faiths Sunday?" he grumbled.

"Please, Father, not in church," his daughter said and she waved at Chaplain Hallowell who colored slightly.

The colonel's daughter was pretty, with dark hair and big dark eyes, but her figure was rather blocky. She wasn't long and light like Ella; not fragile. She reminded me of a nurse we had at Interdom, not the looks—the Interdom nurse was a real battle-ax—but the economy of movement, the kind of efficient way she did common things like sitting down and folding her hands.

Miss Pollard sat between the colonel and Crowell, dividing her attention with an exactitude that was amazing to watch. If she smiled at one, she smiled also at the other. When she spoke to one she delivered the last half of the sentence to the other with remarkable charm and diplomacy.

I was watching this byplay when I felt a tap on my shoulder. "Hey, dog meat."

I looked around to find Laperuta, Powell, Weller and Morgan at the door wearing exaggerated expressions of piety and contrition. "What're you guys doing here?" I asked.

"We've come to cleanse our souls with public confession," Powell said.

"We are sinners," Weller intoned lugubriously.

"Our hearts are black," Morgan said.

"Public confession of what?" I stammered.

"Carnal thoughts about the Girl from Escondido," Laperuta said.

"But that's not done here!" I hissed. "Not in public!"

"I've seen it done lots of times down South," Powell said. "Why, them old men stand right up and rattle off sins of a lifetime, wailin' and carryin' on about their transgressions of the flesh, prouder all the time until they about bust, and then some other old turkey stands up and tries to top him."

"Sure," Weller said. "Them Bible bangers out our way always got time to listen to a good dirty public confession. Why, I heard things said in tent meetings that you couldn't print in France."

"But this isn't a tent meeting!" I said. "It's not that kind of thing."

"We'll make it that kind of thing," Laperuta said.

I broke into a cold sweat. I prayed for a flat tire on Chief Budd's pickup, for a broken gas pump, drive shaft, con rod, anything that wouldn't hurt Ella, but anything to keep her away. "Boys," I whispered hoarsely, "you don't have anything to confess. *I'm* the sinner."

"Impure thoughts," Weller said. "We had impure thoughts about your girl."

"I don't have a girl!"

"We want to come clean," Laperuta said.

"Laperuta, not in church," I said. "Anywhere else, but not in church!"

"I can't think of a better place," he said.

I caught Laperuta's arm. "Max," I begged, "Max, anything you want. Look, I got a little money saved. You can have it. I got—look here, a wristwatch, self-winding, antimagnetic, waterproof, luminous dial . . ."

Laperuta glanced at my watch. "It ain't gold," he said.

"I'll have it plated," I said, "gold plated."

"Let me see it."

I handed my watch to Laperuta. They all looked at it.

"How much cash?" Laperuta asked.

"Eighty-five bucks."

"That don't split four ways. Make it a hundred and I'll think about it," he said.

"Max," I implored. "I don't have any more."

"Well, Danbom, we'll just sit there in church communing about it. We'll try to make up our minds if we can carry this load on our consciences for a hundred bucks."

"A hundred?" I croaked.

"A hundred," he said.

Morgan, Powell and Weller nodded.

"There's just one more thing, Danbom," Laperuta said.

"Yes?" I whispered.

"If you don't want us to make a testimonial, sometime during this service you find a place to stand up and tell everyone what kind of lying virgin you are."

"But I did that!" I protested.

"Not in church you didn't," Weller said. "I ain't goin' to believe it until I hear it in church."

"Weller," I begged. "Believe it!"

"Naw," Weller said, shaking his head. "That girl meant too much to me."

"A bunch of us got together last night," Laperuta said, "and a few of the fats over in A Company decided maybe you said what you said under duress."

"Because we were killing you," Morgan explained.

"So we deputized ourselves to see to it that you made a free confession," Laperuta concluded.

"I'll believe it if I hear it in church," Weller repeated.

"Shut up, Weller," Powell said.

"Laperuta, please," I implored, "you can't make me do this."

"See?" Weller said.

"Will you shut up!" Powell said to Weller.

"That's right, Danbom," Laperuta said piously. "We can't *make* you, but we hope that you'll be stirred to utter the truth. If necessary we'll set you an example. A lot of guys are skeptical, see."

I looked around the chapel and saw that most of the men were watching me.

Chaplain Duff was playing an organ interlude. Chaplain Horowitz, who was going to lead the service and deliver the sermon, was fingering his notes nervously. Chaplain Hallowell alerted his choir to stand by.

The service was about to begin.

I looked back at Laperuta and over his shoulder saw Chief Budd's pickup truck in the street. "All right," I said. "I'll confess again. Go sit down."

Mercifully, I had no time to consider the effect an abrupt public confession of my virginity would have on Ella, because she jumped from the truck and hurried toward me with Chief Budd trailing behind. She was smiling and the sun striking her hair made a golden halo about her head. "Charlie," she called, "are you surprised?" And she rushed into my arms as though she never wanted to leave. "Father Duff called," she said.

Chief Budd scowled at me. "When I see it I'll believe it," he said.

I handed the chief an order of service. Hallowell's choir began to sing. Ella took my arm and led me toward the center aisle. "Hurry," she whispered, "they're starting."

I walked down the aisle with Ella on my arm and Chief Budd shuffling along behind us reading the program notes. Crosscurrents and riptides were running in my brain and for a minute I thought I was going to psych out. Ella was there and I was happy, but because she was there I was miserable.

Chaplain Horowitz looked up, saw us, and fumbled his notes. Chaplain Duff missed a chord on the organ as he half rose to get a glimpse of Ella. The choir was singing boldly but I'd heard the words so often in rehearsal that at first they didn't register:

> "Turn back, O man, forswear thy foolish ways,
> Old now is earth and none may count her days,
> Yet thou, her child, whose head is crowned with flame
> Still will not hear thine inner God proclaim:
> Turn back, O man, forswear thy foolish ways."

Suddenly Weller stood straight up, his jaw gaping, his eyes riveted on Ella. Then I saw that every man in the chapel was staring at her as though Saint Joan had appeared to them in shining armor.

"Doves' eyes within her locks," Morgan exclaimed.

"That dirty Danbom was lying about lying!" Powell cried.

They thought Ella was the Girl from Escondido!

I caught Ella's arm and turned back.

"What is it, Charlie?" she asked. "Am I unfastened, or something?"

She reached for the zipper at the back of her dress, but I hustled her up the aisle, brushing Chief Budd aside as we passed him.

"Hey!" he said.

"Wrong church," I said.

"What do you mean wrong church?"

"Wrong day, I mean. I mean wrong day."

We reached the door and Ella balked. "Charlie! What's wrong with you?"

I glanced back and saw Weller shambling up the aisle with a catatonic expression on his face. "Stature like a palm tree," he mumbled. "Joints like jewels."

The boys rose and followed him.

I decided to make my stand at the door. I pushed Ella and the chief through, slammed the door and held it shut from the outside. "Chief," I said, "get her out of this."

"I told her not to get into it in the first place."

Weller began pounding on the door.

"Charlie! What is it?" Ella demanded.

They were pulling at the door. I couldn't hold it. "Ella. I'll explain."

"Do, Charlie, please!" she said.

The racket inside increased. "Charlie's got the Girl from Escondido out there," Weller cried, "in the flesh."

Ella looked at me and I shriveled.

"Escondido!" Chief Budd cried. "The dirty creep has a girl in Escondido! You should have known when Farragut bit him!"

The chief cocked his arm, but before he could strike, the door was forced open and a mass of men boiled out. I tried to hold them. "Run, Ella!" I yelled.

Seeing their crazed expressions, Chief Budd snatched Ella's hand and made a beeline for his pickup truck. I sent Weller sprawling, then fought a delaying action, but I was lifted bodily and carried backward down the path as the whole chapel emptied out. The men were shouting. Some of them knew Ella was the Girl from Escondido, some of them thought she wasn't, some of them thought she was a movie starlet. "That's the girl that bit him," Morgan yelled.

"Good glory, look at them pretty teeth!"

I was thrown down and trampled underfoot. I heard Chief Budd cursing and the starter of his pickup grinding. Marines milled around the truck. Ella was in the cab, but she was frightened. She was crying.

I leaped up and charged Laperuta, Powell, Weller and Morgan. I flailed, slugged, kicked, tossed Morgan over my shoulder, hit Powell clean right between the eyes and saw him stagger. I turned and chopped Laperuta two roundhouse blows that snapped his head like a swing door.

I heard howls, felt crushing blows, felt hands tearing at me, heard screaming. I was exultant. My one aim was to kill Laperuta, Powell, Weller and Morgan.

Every time Laperuta's face swung into view I smashed it. I saw Sergeant Brody and sent him sprawling. I was the Whirlwind of the Lord going forth in fury, falling with pain on the heads of the wicked. Nothing could stop me. Every time I hit a face, a shoulder, a stomach, a chest, the strength of my arms increased. My shirt was torn from my back. Blood from my nose coursed down my face. They brought me to the ground twice, but I rose up and fought. I heard the pickup truck kick over and race away. I cocked my arm and through glazed eyes searched out a target.

Colonel Pollard was directly in front of me.

My arm locked.

In the corner of my swollen eye I saw the smashed dial of my watch. It was twelve past twelve. I heard a gentle spang deep in my skull, like the mainspring of a self-winding, antimagnetic, waterproof, twelve-dollar watch letting go. I fell and the watch works sprinkled over my face, little wheels, cogs, springs and broken crystal.

I heard Colonel Pollard's voice distantly. "Captain Crowell, arrest these men!" he said.

"It's not her!" I yelled, but my throat was blocked and the words stayed in my head, coursing around and around like in an echo chamber. "It's not her, her, her!"

Rough hands seized me and I twisted away, rolling, only semiconscious. "Chaplains!" I yelled. "There is no Girl from Escondido, dido, dido!"

They caught me, my head dangling like a leaf on a broken twig. I saw the sun bobbing in the sky. It smiled a wholesome, toothy, cardboard smile and I blacked out deep and mercifully and the lost boys carried me away from the swip-swop teeth of the gnashing crocodile to where Wendy was waiting.

Eight

WHEN I woke up, I was lying on a table in the brig infirmary. They'd sponged the blood off my face and staunched my broken nose. One eye was shut, but dimly through the other I saw the triad faces of Chaplains Hallowell, Horowitz and Duff.

"Where am I?" I asked.

"The brig," they said.

"How long will I be here?"

"Danbom," Hallowell said, "don't think about that now."

"They'll take good care of you, Danbom," Horowitz said. "The rabies series will take a little while."

"Rabies? What rabies?" I asked.

"The bite on your shoulder," Hallowell said.

"The human bite is very dangerous, Danbom," Duff said. "More dangerous than any animal."

"That's my bite!" I protested. "I'm immune!"

They nodded all three. "Yes, yes," they said compassionately.

"I bit myself," I said. "That was part of it. To make the guys believe she was real."

"But she is," Duff said.

"No, the other one. Ask Strand. He saw me do it."

They nodded, but with no conviction. They didn't believe me.

"Danbom," Hallowell said, "there's going to be a court-martial. Since you're our assistant, we've decided to act as counsel for your defense."

"Oh, please, don't," I said.

"We feel responsible," Duff said. "If I hadn't invited her to come none of this would have happened."

"If you hadn't tipped them off about the Song of Solomon none of this would have happened," I said.

"Solomon is public domain," Horowitz said.

"I've always thought it should have been put in the Apocrypha," Duff said.

"Look, will one of you please call Ella and tell her there is no Girl from Escondido? She'd believe you."

They looked sclf-conscious.

"I called," Duff said, "and got Chief Budd. He was quite irate. Miss Budd wouldn't speak to me. They both believe you have a girl in Escondido. Half this battalion believes you have a girl in Escondido. Tell us her name, Danbom."

"How can she have a name if she doesn't exist!" I cried.

"We'll look her up and if she isn't there we'll know," Hallowell said.

I closed my eyes and moaned. I was lost. The girl I had created out of virgin desperation, out of movie posters, swimsuit signs, deodorant ads, perfume layouts, corset, brassiere, stocking, hairnet, wave set, lady razor blade jingles, made of neon, made of plaster, alabaster, newsprint and the Song of Solomon was larger than life. She was indestructible and she had me in her fleshless embrace.

When the chaplains left I was moved to a cell where I lay all night tormented by dreams of my creation.

She came in many guises. Starting as a pinpoint Venus in the sky, she came toward me growing larger and more horrible with hair like goats, teeth like sheep, her garments smelling of Lebanon, her eyes like the fishpools of Heshbon, her nose a tower of apples, and she would crush down on me and plant her branding lips on my bitten shoulder.

Or I would start awake and find only her head above me, Medusa, snake-wreathed, popping contact lenses out of her eyes like tears, their color changing from green to red, to gold, and the lenses falling on my chest like hot crystal from the face of a shattered watch.

The next morning I was shocked by my gaunt, haunted appearance. The creature had occupied me. I saw her staring out of my own eyes at my wretched face in the mirror.

The brig guard came and looked in at me suspiciously. "You nuts, Danbom," he asked, "or are you just putting it on?"

"I'm nuts," I said.

"How does it feel?" he asked.

"Like firecrackers at Christmas," I said. "Call me an exorcist."

The guard shook his head wonderingly and went away.

At ten o'clock the chaplains came to confer about their plans for my defense. Fifteen men had been arrested for fighting in front of the church. Colonel Pollard had scheduled a summary court to try these offenders; among them were Laperuta, Powell, Weller, Morgan and several men from Crowell's company, including two members of the choir. The chaplains had questioned several of the defendants and found a certain amount of confusion.

Two A Company men claimed to have thought the chapel was on fire. Another said he'd run outside to stop the fight. Two thought Ella was an actress. One said he thought she was his sister. The H and S Company men were convinced that Ella was the Girl from Escondido.

"But you could prove who Ella is if you brought her here," I said.

"We don't have the power of subpoena and she won't talk to us," Duff said.

"The chief has threatened physical violence," Hallowell said.

"All right, what can they do to me?" I asked.

"You could forfeit a month's pay," Hallowell said.

"And get restricted."

"And extra duty."

"That's not so bad," I said despondently.

"But that's not the point," Horowitz said.

"The point," Duff said, "is that we chaplains are here as guests of a sister service."

"Brother service," Horowitz said.

"What's the difference? Sister. Brother."

"There is a difference," Horowitz said.

"I know the difference," Duff retorted.

"I don't think the Marines like to be called sisters."

"All right, *brother* service," Duff said.

"As you know, Danbom," Hallowell said, "there isn't a great deal of love lost between the Navy and the Marine Corps. We're in trouble. In fact, this whole Chaplain Reserve training program is in trouble. Chaplain Bernard had us on the mat. Chief Budd lodged a complaint with the provost marshal against the unprovoked attack on his niece. This thing has gone up to Division and the general isn't pleased."

"Colonel Pollard is displeased," Duff said.

"But they can't blame you. I started the fight."

"You're our assistant," Horowitz said. "The fight started during our service, which doesn't say much about our ability as purveyors of peace and goodwill. Right now, we're mud. We're fat, and by association every chaplain on this base is fat."

"Okay," I said. "What time is the court-martial?"

"Sixteen hundred in the colonel's office," Hallowell said.

At sixteen hundred, Sergeant Strand marched us into the office where we stood like fifteen statues in front of the colonel's desk. The chaplains and Captain Crowell were there and Chaplain Hallowell was making a statement.

On a table in one corner of the office was a large sandbox with the topographical features of Camp Pendleton in damp sand. In some places there were plow marks in the sand, probably left by the colonel's swagger stick as he worked out tactical problems. There was a picture of Miss Pollard on the desk and the colonel often glanced at it as he listened.

"So with that as a prologue and an apology, sir," Chaplain Hallowell was saying, "I'd like Chaplain Horowitz to describe the background of this case."

Horowitz began to describe the background. He'd been over my records and made a phone call to Interdom to get character references. He'd spoken to a Pastor Darlington who was new there and didn't know me, but Brother Queen remembered me as a skinny, incorrigible, tone deaf boy who had steadfastly refused to accept religious guidance.

I saw a flicker of interest in Colonel Pollard's eye. He glanced at me with something akin to approval and told Horowitz to get on with it.

"The point, sir, is that through no fault of his own, this boy has been institutionalized all his life. He has lived almost exclusively in an all-male society which accounts for why he bit himself."

"What's that?" Colonel Pollard asked sharply.

"He bit himself, sir, to prove that he had a girl. You see, sir, Danbom has never had a girl and that puts him at a distinct disadvantage among the other men."

"And you say he bit himself?" Pollard asked again.

"Yes, sir," Horowitz said. "Sergeant Strand witnessed it."

Colonel Pollard glanced at Strand. "Strand?" he asked.

"Yes, sir," Strand replied smartly. "I saw him do it."

The colonel's face got a little tighter.

"So you see, Colonel," Horowitz continued, "from this we deduce that the Girl from Escondido is not real."

"Oh, you do, do you?" the colonel said.

"Certainly, sir. The only real evidence she existed was Danbom's bite which was self-inflicted. If the bite is false, the teeth are false, ergo the girl is false, which proves Private Danbom was lying about her in order to conceal the fact that he is a virgin."

"Is that so?" the colonel said.

Chaplain Duff stepped forward. "Of course, sir," he said. "You see everyone assumed, because of the bite, that she was a somewhat carnal person and that Danbom had known her."

"Known her?" the colonel said.

"Carnally, sir," Chaplain Duff explained.

"She was what is known as a toothsome bit, sir," Chaplain Hallowell said.

"A false toothsome bit," Horowitz amended.

Colonel Pollard seized his swagger stick and his knuckles turned white as he gripped it. "And you say he took her description from the Song of Solomon?" he asked with animus glittering in his eyes.

"Only partially, sir," Hallowell interjected. "We find, upon reconstruction, that he got part of her description from a Trans-World Airlines poster, a manikin of a stewardess and fragments of various advertisements."

"Is that so?" the colonel said.

"Also dog hair," Duff added.

"Dog hair?" Pollard said, trembling slightly.

"Yes, from a cocker spaniel named Farragut owned by Chief Budd. Private Weller has it in his wallet. The hair, I mean."

Weller's face colored with righteous indignation. "That

hair in my wallet is from the Girl from Escondido," he declared. "I seen her with my own eyes and I knew all along Danbom was lying about lying."

"Quiet there," Strand growled.

"Perhaps we could, ah, request the dog to appear," Hallowell suggested.

Pollard nodded agreeably. "Or we could wire J. Edgar Hoover and have the FBI run tests on this hair to find out where it's from."

"Why, yes," Hallowell said beaming brightly.

The colonel's swagger stick slashed a chip off the corner of his desk. Sawop! "My guess," he seethed, "is that the report would show the hair to be from a ring-tailed theological baboon!"

Weller groaned.

"Now, sir," Duff said, "the point we're trying to make is that this young Marine was forced by the—ah—common mores and expectations of barracks life, to conceal his virginal condition in order to retain the respect of his mates—ah, friends. It seems there is a stigma attached to being—with the exception of priests like myself—to being inexperienced with respect to women. This is a sad fact, but a true one. Now the confusion here came about because this young man found a real girl and, naturally, he was anxious to protect her reputation and to distinguish her from his other girl . . ."

"Which girl?" Pollard asked.

"The Girl from Escondido, sir," Duff said, glancing at Horowitz for corroboration.

"Yes, sir," Horowitz said. "The Girl from Escondido."

"Who doesn't exist," Pollard said.

The chaplains smiled and nodded.

"That's right," Hallowell said.

Colonel Pollard's tense face took on a darker hue. He rose. "This," he said, "is the fattest thing I have ever heard. It is pig fat, chicken fat, lard. It is grease! There was a brawl in front of our chapel. A young girl was insulted. Your assistant was involved and these men contributed to the fracas. There seems to be a division of opinion here as to who in hell is who and who is a virgin, or not. But I can tell you right now that I couldn't care less. What in hell do you think I'm running here—a finishing school for idiots? Captain Crowell, do you have anything to say before I pass sentence?"

"Well, sir—" Captain Crowell said.

"Well, sir, what!" Pollard hissed and he slapped the desk with his swagger stick.

"Well, sir, there does seem to be some relationship between virginity and the moral fiber and stamina of the men. It seems that the men in the ranks have a certain respect for the—the experienced man. I've noticed it, sir. A man who had a few girls stashed around seems to command attention."

"That cuts it, Crowell!" Pollard exclaimed. "That tears it. Do you mean to say that advancement in the Corps depends on sexual experience?"

"I wouldn't put it that baldly, sir," Crowell said.

"How in hell baldly would you put it?" Pollard demanded.

"I'd say it's a factor which heretofore has not been taken into consideration," Crowell said.

"Heretofore," Pollard shot back.

"Yes, sir," Crowell said.

"Well, let's take it into consideration," Pollard declared. "Let's take it into consideration right here and now."

"Yes, sir," Crowell said.

Colonel Pollard scanned us, then he slapped his swagger stick down. "Every virgin in the room, one pace forward," he commanded.

The order hit us cold. I hesitated, but saw the chaplains' eyes fixed on me. I stepped forward one pace.

For a moment I was alone, then the men from Crowell's company stepped forward, one at a time, all seven of them.

Duff took one pace forward.

Corporal Laperuta was so shocked that he stepped back one pace.

Chaplain Hallowell tottered, then he too stepped forward to stand beside Duff.

"I've got a wife and three kids, Colonel," Horowitz said.

Colonel Pollard's eyes swung to Captain Crowell. "Did I see you move, sir?" he demanded.

Crowell turned crimson. "A side step, sir," he said.

"Fat!" Pollard spat. He looked down the broken line, deliberating. "Captain Crowell," he said presently, "there is a problem to which I have been giving a great deal of consideration lately."

"Yes, sir?" Crowell said.

"I've been trying to decide the code names for the coming exercise."

"Yes, sir," Crowell said. "We've been waiting to hear."

"Tell me, Captain, do you believe the Girl from Escondido is an actual person, or not?"

"What, sir?"

"The question is simple enough, Captain. Do you believe there is a Girl from Escondido?"

"No, sir," Captain Crowell said.

Colonel Pollard smiled icily. "Very well, then," he said. "For our field exercise next week, your company will be known as the Virgins. H and S Company will be the Escondidos. Did you get that?"

"Yes, Colonel," Crowell said miserably.

"And since you and the chaplains seem so well attuned, I'm going to attach them and their assistant to your company for the remainder of their stay on this base. Do you have any objection?"

Captain Crowell looked at the chaplains and shook his head like a lost soul. "No, Colonel," he whispered.

"And now," Colonel Pollard said turning to us, "you men, virgins or not, will each forfeit two weeks' pay and be given two hours extra duty per day for one month. Do any of you wish to appeal?"

No one moved.

"Is that satisfactory with you chaplains?" Pollard demanded.

Chaplains Hallowell, Horowitz and Duff nodded bleakly.

"Dismissed," Pollard said.

That evening the chaplains and I loaded our gear into the Fat Wagon and tried to get clear of H and S Company under cover of darkness, but unfortunately the boys had organized a send-off. Men spilled out of the huts and lined the street as we drove away.

"Go, fats, go!" they yelled. "So long, virgins!"

I saw Strand's cigar flare in the darkness, illuminating the reptilian grin on his face.

"Sing us the Song of Solomon, Danbom," Laperuta yelled. There was a barrage of laughter and it was obvious to me that Laperuta was once again head tail man in the battalion.

On the way to the A Company area, the chaplains maintained a martyred silence. We weren't expecting a welcome, for along with ourselves and our gear we brought the disgrace of the code name Virgins.

Staff Sergeant Jackson of A Company Headquarters met us. A paunchy Negro with a comforting grin and a good baritone voice, he hopped onto the running board and guided us to our new hut. He bent down and looked at the chaplains. "I got an idea how you feel," he said. "Just like colored in an all-white school."

"That's precisely it," Chaplain Duff said.

"Don't you worry," Jackson said. "They can call us fats or virgins or any damned thing they want, this is still the best rifle company in the battalion. Here we are."

Jackson swung off the Fat Wagon and I stopped. We followed him into a hut where we found a dozen men waiting for us. Thinking it was a goon squad, I panicked, but before I could bolt through the door the men began to sing.

It just about knocked me flat.

Sergeant Jackson joined in, his big voice booming through the hut: "O de gospel train's a'comin'—I hear it just at han',—I hear de car wheels rumblin'—an' rollin' thro' de lan'. Git on board, little children. Git on board, little children."

The chaplains were dumbfounded.

Sergeant Jackson began to clap his hands and march with the A Company choir members rocking, clapping and singing as they circled us. It was wild.

Sergeant Jackson passed us and winked. "When the fat's in the fire," he said, "what you need is Ministers of the Lard!"

Jackson laughed, the men laughed and presently the chaplains laughed too.

"Ministers of the Lard!" Duff cried. "We'll do the best we can."

The A Company men were, indeed, heavier than those in H and S, but their comportment tended to corroborate the old saw that fat men are happy men. At least they were enthusiastic. When they'd finished singing they stood around us grinning, and Jackson made a speech.

"Welcome, rejects," Jackson said. "This company may not be lean, but we got guts." He patted his paunch and chuckled. "If fighting men travel on their stomachs we'll go a long way. If we can't walk we'll roll. Now I don't much get the drift of this virgin thing. In my book if you are, you are, if you ain't you can't go back to it. I heard a lot of talk right here in this outfit about the Girl from Escondido. Down here, of course, she's a good deal heftier than she was over at H and S; we go on the theory that there can't be too much of a good thing.

"Be that as it may, this company has been taking the butt end of the colonel's swagger stick for a long time now. Part is because the Old Man and Captain Crowell have locked horns over training procedures. The Old Man is of the misery school, the wipe-that-smile-off-your-face school, the school that says angry men fight better than happy men. Part is because our captain is planning to marry the only apple of the colonel's eye.

"Now I've heard from Strand, and Brody, and from the captain himself that you chaplains, and you, Danbom, have sent the Old Man home nearly every night with his shins black-and-blue from thrashing them with his swagger stick. You have, in short, fouled up, royally. Meaning no disrespect to the clergy, I'm going to put you people on notice. We may be fats, but we're not fools. We'll cover for you when we can, we'll help all we can, but we're heading into an exercise next week that's going to take the best every man in this outfit can give. Now, in order for us to come off as Captain Crowell wants us to we're going to have to sharp up. We don't want to borrow trouble, or make trouble. In this outfit we work together. Okay?"

The chaplains nodded, sincerely. I did too.

Jackson smiled and offered his hand. "Welcome to A Company," he said.

The chaplains shook Jackson's hand and the men helped us move our gear into the hut.

The next afternoon I reported to Sergeant Jackson for extra duty. He handed me a gunnysack and a broomstick with a nail in the end of it. "There's a four-mile stretch of road from here to the Pacific Coast Highway, Danbom. You go out and pick up the gum wrappers, beer cans and bottles along the right-of-way. You can keep all the returns you find, maybe they'll make up for the loss in your pay."

"Right, Sarge," I said.

Five minutes later I was poking along the road thinking about Ella, thinking I'd probably spend my declining years as a derelict living out of garbage cans, when a Plymouth convertible came toward me. A girl was driving and for a moment I thought I was hallucinating again. I closed my eyes and was relieved when the car and driver disappeared, but I heard it come to a stop and a voice: "Private Danbom?"

There was enough presence in the voice to distinguish it from those I'd heard in dreams so I opened my eyes and saw Miss Pollard. "Yes?" I said.

"I'm Brandy Pollard," she said.

"Yes, ma'am, I know."

"I've been working on your case," she said and she smiled cordially. "Chaplain Hallowell asked me to help out."

"I didn't know that," I said.

"It's a very interesting case," she said. "I majored in sociology."

"Everything is pretty fouled up," I said.

"Yes," she said, "it is." She cut the motor and slid toward me across the seat. "Do you have time to talk?"

I looked down the road both ways. It was clear. "I guess so," I said.

She seemed hesitant, then she sighed. "I will confess that at first this didn't make much sense to me," she said, "but since yesterday I've taken a personal interest."

"I appreciate that, ma'am," I said.

"A personal self-interest," she added and looked straight into my eyes. "Tell me something, will you, Charles?"

Her direct manner and the note of appeal in her voice puzzled me. "What, ma'am?" I asked.

"Father told me about the summary court yesterday, but I'd like another viewpoint."

"Well, ma'am, I was scared all the time," I said.

She nodded. "I suppose so, but when Father asked the virgins to step forward, did Captain Crowell move?"

The question took me off guard. The possibilities were numerous. I hadn't seen Captain Crowell move, but I remembered him saying he'd stepped to the side. If he wasn't a virgin it could be on Miss Pollard's account, then again it couldn't. I thought I'd better dummy up.

"Father said he didn't," Miss Pollard said.

"Well, ma'am, I had my eyes front. We were at attention."

"Out of the corner of your eye, Charles?" she asked. "You must have seen something."

"Well, ma'am, the colonel asked the captain if he'd moved and the captain said he'd stepped to the side."

She looked puzzled. "How would you interpret that?" she asked.

"I'd say he sidestepped the question, ma'am."

She was bemused. "Interesting," she said presently.

"Miss Pollard," I said, "I sure wouldn't want to get into any trouble with Captain Crowell."

"He'll never know I spoke to you."

"Thank you, ma'am."

"And Chaplain Hallowell stepped forward?"

"Yes, ma'am. He did."

"Amazing," she said. Then she looked directly at me

again. "I'm afraid I've got some bad news for you, Charles," she said. "Chief Budd has been transferred to Okinawa. He's going to sell the motel and Ella is going to her mother in Orlando."

"Orlando, Florida?"

Miss Pollard nodded. "She's leaving next week."

All the color seemed to go out of the hills. There weren't any birds singing and no breeze stirring the grass. Everything stuck, black and white, like a dead picture in my mind. "You talked to her?" I asked.

"Yes, I went to the motel."

"Did she mention me?"

"You're all we talked about," Miss Pollard said. "She was shocked, of course, to discover your association with the other girl."

"But you told her there's no other girl. You told her that, didn't you?"

Miss Pollard frowned. "Well, Charles," she said, "I don't know if I did the right thing or not. I had to play it by ear, you see. She's a very nice girl. A pretty girl."

"Yes, I know!"

"But she *is* a girl. We talked for a good long time and I finally decided not to tell her."

"Not to tell her!" I cried. "But you're the only one she'll talk to! The chaplains have tried, but she won't listen to them."

Miss Pollard nodded. "But, Charles, your story is slightly incredible, isn't it?" she asked. "I mean the Song of Solomon and you biting yourself on the shoulder. That's hard to swallow, wouldn't you think? I'd have had to tell her all that, bite included, and I suppose the circumstances under which a young man gets bitten on the shoulder are, to say the least, intimate."

"I did it in the shower," I said.

"Yes, but where did she do it?"

"Who?" I asked.

"Your girl in Escondido."

"But there is no—"

"But Ella thinks there is. And all things considered, Charles, I think it's better for her to continue thinking so."

"But then I'm right back where I started!"

"Not quite," Miss Pollard said. "I told Ella you liked her better than your other girl and she was flattered."

"But I don't have another girl."

"Charles!" Miss Pollard said impatiently. "Will you please listen? I know more about women than you do. I am one."

"Yes, ma'am," I said.

"We're vain and we're jealous, so the notion that you preferred her to the Girl from Escondido, a girl I took some pains to point out was the idol of a whole battalion of Marines, pleased her vanity. I think if you call Ella she'll listen. Of course she'll have to pretend a certain indifference to spare her pride, but she will listen."

"Do you mean I have to pretend that I had a girl in Escondido?"

"I strongly advise that you do so," Miss Pollard said. "But that, of course, is up to you." Then she slid back behind the wheel, started the car and drove away.

When she was out of earshot I slammed my broomstick spear into the ground and cursed.

It was awful! I'd sworn off lying and pretending. I'd gone through the disgrace of exposure, through fire and ostracism. I'd been court-martialed, publicly shamed. I'd admitted I was a liar and a virgin and managed, by sacrificing my reputation, to reduce belief in the Girl from Escondido from a hundred percent to almost nothing. True, there were a few diehards, like Weller, but I didn't care about them. But Ella! To have her still believing meant that the Girl from Escondido was perceived and therefore continued to exist. The one person I cared for, my own Ella, was maintaining the existence of that dog, that trollop born of my imagination. It was terrible.

I stabbed candy wrappers and newspapers on the way back to camp, trying to decide what to do. Halfway there I realized that I couldn't clearly recall Ella's face. It seemed an age since I'd seen her and she was going to Orlando! She was turning into cardboard!

I ran.

The wind made my eyes smart. I gulped air like a fish out of water and my feet slapped the hot pavement. I was terrified. I got to the phone booth in the parking lot and fell inside, panting. I had to save her face, and to do that I had to hear her voice. My hands trembled as I dialed the Admiral Motel. I got the chief.

"Hello, Chief, this is Charlie Danbom," I said.

"By golly," Budd cawed, "if it ain't the Casanova kid! The squire of Escondido, the maiden's terror."

"Chief, you sound intoxicated."

"You're bloody damned tootin' I'm intoxicated," Budd crowed. "Not only that, I'm drunk!"

"Who is it?" I heard Ella said.

"It's that damn bum Danbom. Hey, Danbom, how do you spell Schweitzer?"

"Schweitzer?"

"Ghandi then. You're the religious type."

Budd had a fit of howling laughter.

"Let me talk to him," I heard Ella say.

"Sure, give him hell, Ella. Smoke him up good."

"You go out and paint some more," Ella said.

"How do you spell Dag Hammarskjöld?" Budd asked.

Ella spelled it and I heard the chief blunder outside and the door slam shut behind him. "Come on, Lord Russell," he called and Farragut barked.

"Admiral Motel," Ella said, very businesslike.

"This is Charlie Danbom," I said.

"Oh, yes, Mr. Danbom. How are you?"

"This is Charlie," I said.

"Yes, I know."

There was a pause but her face came back to me, she was real again.

"Ella," I said, "it's me."

"I'm aware of that," she said.

"I had a talk with Miss Pollard today," I said.

"So did I."

"She said I maybe ought to call you."

"Oh, did she?"

"So I called."

"I see you have."

The operator asked for another quarter. I heard the coin drop and bells. "Hello, Ella?"

"Admiral Motel," she said.

"Ella, I called to apologize and explain."

"Heavens, what is there to explain?" she said with a sound in her voice like dill pickles. "It's perfectly obvious, isn't it?"

"Well, that's what I called about," I said. "The situation is a little confused. I wanted to clear it up."

"You'd better hurry, or it'll cost you another quarter," she said.

"I don't mind," I said. "I've got a pocketful of change."

"I suppose so, with all the calls you must make."

"What calls?" I asked.

"How much is a toll call to Escondido?"

"I don't know," I said.

"Oh, I suppose you call her collect. Well, I do wish you'd thrown a little of your business our way, Charles."

"What business, Ella? Listen, I want to talk to you."

"Why, your motel business, of course. Surely you provided bed and shelter, or is she the back seat type?"

"Ella, you're twice the girl she'll ever be! You know that!"

"I'm sure," she said with cat claws in her voice.

"Three times," I said. "Ella, I love you. I really do. I don't care if I ever see her again."

"Neither do I," she said, her voice softening just a touch. "But I'm sure what I think makes no difference to you."

"Ella, I've got to see you."

"Did Miss Pollard tell you I was leaving?"

"Yes."

"The motel is up for sale."

"I know. But, Ella, please, don't go."

"I don't have any choice, Charlie," she said and she was herself again. I nearly fell down with happiness. "I have to go somewhere," she said.

"Why can't you stay there?"

"Because single girls can't run motels. It's a rule of the world, or something. I told Uncle Budd I could manage it while he was gone, but he just hit the ceiling and said he'd burn it down before he'd leave me to all those Marine wolves who roam the beach. He got really mad!"

"But Orlando is a million miles away."

"I don't want to go, Charlie, but what can I do?"

I was home again. I had a girl, a real girl, asking my advice. "Ella," I said. "I want you to listen to me. I love you. I want to marry you. I want to start off with you honest all around, you know?"

"Yes?" she said.

"Ella," I said, "you're the only girl I've ever had in this world, so help me God. The Girl from Escondido was just a lie. She never was real, Ella. Do you understand?"

There was a pause, then Ella's voice came back like icicles. "Charles Danbom," she said, "if you think you can continue to two-time me you're sadly mistaken. You're not the only fish in the sea and don't you forget it! Everybody knows about that other creature so don't lie to me." She started crying. "I'd hoped, stupidly I see now, that you'd given her up, but I see you haven't. Good-bye forever, Mr. Danbom. I'm going to Orlando and you know where you can go and I hope you'll be happy with her!"

"Ella!" I called.

She was still there, sobbing and trying not to let me hear it.

"Ella! I'm telling you the truth!"

She hung up.

For a long time I stood there in that coffin booth, benumbed by the realization that it was about as foolish for me to deny the existence of the Girl from Escondido as it was to deny the existence of God.

Fictions have a life of their own and if they're any good there isn't much can kill them. Somebody is always going to clap for Tinker Bell and groan with Lear and weep for Little Dorrit. I'd tried to tell Ella the truth and what chance did it have? There was a girl in Escondido and her lungs weren't very good, but she was going to Orlando, Florida, for the cure. She had a lovely cardboard face and an uncle in the Navy and an imaginary boyfriend named me.

I wandered back to the hut I shared with the chaplains.

They observed my condition without comment.

"Chaplains," I said, "tell me something."

"Yes?" they said.

"Anything," I said.

"What do you mean?" Hallowell asked.

I sat down on my bunk with the gunnysack of candy wrappers still slung over my shoulder and the broomstick scepter in my hand. "That," I said, "is what I'm trying to find out."

"Ah, yes," they said and they nodded.

Nine

THE next day we got an order to stencil the six-inch letter V on our helmet liners in white phosphorescent paint. This was to distinguish us from the H and S Company Escondidos who would wear their field caps during the maneuver.

I fell in line to draw a stencil and paint to decorate the chaplains' helmet liners and overheard Sergeant Jackson telling the men that Captain Crowell would prefer us to think of ourselves as the Vth Provisional Marine Brigade for purposes of the exercise. Crowell didn't care what they called us at Battalion H. Q., or at Division, but for himself he had some misgivings about leading Virgins in battle.

Jackson's suggestion wasn't well received.

"Fat Stick stuck us with the name and we'll keep it," one man called.

"I may not qualify," another said, "but a lot of Escondidos do if they'd come clean."

"Esprit the Corps and screw the Escondidos."

Jackson shrugged and told them to have it their way, but not to let Captain Crowell know how they felt about it.

Colonel Pollard was determined to make the maneuver a lively one, with simulated mine fields, artillery fire and night marches. His training methods had captured the attention of the division general, who was particularly interested in Pollard's claim that the First Battalion could move troops faster, through rough terrain in a tactical situation and without motor transport, than any other battalion in the division.

This assertion focused attention on the coming exercise. The Marine Corps spent millions of dollars each year developing, testing and equipping its fighting units with troop carriers, trucks, tanks, helicopters, mechanical mules, and treaded vehicles of all sorts. Colonel Pollard claimed that the number of men it took to service and operate these vehicles sapped the fighting vitality of a battalion, that with all the emphasis on mechanization the Marine Corps had lost its capacity to move and to fight on foot. Pollard claimed that without vehicles and all the gewgaws and gadgets that had come into the Corps, he could put more troops on the firing line. His dictum—if you can't carry it, eat it, or shoot it, don't bring it—had begun to win adherents in high places and the Virgin-Escondido exercise was going to effect some important decisions.

As I walked back to the hut with my stencil and paint I gave some serious thought to the new fiction which was growing up around me—the fiction of deep enmity between the Virgins and the Escondidos.

I felt it taking hold myself as I painted the symbol on

our helmet liners. The white V provoked me and yet I wanted to defend it, even to the point of doing bodily harm to those who threatened it. It wasn't logical; it was just a feeling, but it was genuine.

We weren't sure when the exercise would start; we were on standby, expected to be ready any time, but the longer we waited the deeper our antipathy toward the Escondidos took root.

Captain Crowell had been hustling A Company for three solid days. He wore a look of pinched concentration and the lights in his office burned late as he pored over grid maps of the area through which we were to fight.

The sergeants consistently referred to the Escondidos with a list of pungent epithets which grew longer and more flavorful with each passing day.

It was the same on the other side.

One night a group of Escondidos slipped into the Virgin area and turned a fire hose on a hut full of sleeping men.

The Virgins retaliated the next night with two G. I. cans full of slops carefully selected for their viscosity and stench.

There were minor forays, fistfights and threats of extinction which kept us keyed up and sleeping lightly.

I finished stenciling the helmet liners, set them out to dry and thought about calling Ella again. For the last day and a half, since our fatal conversation, I'd been trying to think of something that might possibly save our relationship. I couldn't believe it was finished—not really. But I didn't know what to do. The sound of the receiver banging down when she hung up was still blunt as a blackjack in my ear.

All I could think of was that she was going, going, going

to Orlando. It was a refrain which pierced all my extra-duty candy wrappers and filled my gunnysack with woe. She was going to Orlando because I'd told her the truth and she thought it a lie.

There is no appeal from that. None, except that I tell her a lie and assume she'd think I was telling the truth. But I didn't want to make Ella the patsy of my imagination. I didn't want a relationship based on a falsification, but she was going!

In desperation I left the helmet liners drying on the step, called Miss Pollard and told her what I had done.

"Oh, dear," she said. "I warned you."

"I know, ma'am," I said, "but I thought honesty was the best policy."

"Where did you learn that?" she asked.

"I don't remember," I said. "I guess it just came out of the air."

"Yes, those things do," she said despairingly. "Well, Charles, if you're going to go around telling the truth after being such a good liar, you're really going to make trouble for yourself."

"I suppose so," I said.

"Behind every great truth there's a lie, Charles, just as behind every great man there's a woman."

"But I'm sick of lying!" I protested. "I wanted to be honest with Ella. What's wrong with that?"

"The thing that's wrong, Charles, is that Ella is a very romantic girl. Most of us are. We like to think that a man is willing to make some sacrifice for us, don't you see?"

"I'll do that," I said. "I'm willing to do that."

"Yes, but what can you sacrifice for Ella if your other

girl isn't real? Don't you see, Charles, what you said to Ella, in effect, was that you were willing to give up nothing for her."

"I'm willing to give up everything for her!"

"That's no good either," Miss Pollard said. "It has to be something."

"Miss Pollard!" I implored. "What can I do?"

"You're scheduled for maneuvers, aren't you?"

"Yes, and she's going to Orlando."

Miss Pollard thought, then she sighed. "I really am sorry, Charles. Really I am. And it would have worked out so nicely too. If Ella would marry you then she could manage the motel while the chief was gone, which I'm sure would have pleased him very much."

"I don't want her to marry me to save the motel," I protested. "I want her to love me."

"She does love you, silly," Miss Pollard said irritably. "Of course she does. That's the simplest part of it. But how can she prove it to you?"

"I'll take her word for it!"

"No, Charlie. The way she'll prove it is by forgiving you."

"For what?" I cried.

"For your relationship to the Girl from Escondido."

I moaned. I stood there in that phone booth and my heart broke like shattering glass. "Thank you, Miss Pollard," I blubbered. "Thank you very much."

"I'm sorry, Charles," she said. "I wish there was something I could do, but right now I can't think what it would be."

When I got back to the hut the four helmet liners were

gone from the step and instantly I assumed the Escondidos had swiped them.

I stopped dead and looked around, then I caught myself, alarmed to think that here, while I was facing a real problem, I had been seduced into believing that four lousy helmet liners would attract the Escondidos.

I spoke to myself aloud. "Danbom," I said, "you're suffering from quicksand of the mind."

I went into the hut and found the chaplains. They had their helmet liners. Mine was on my bunk, the V glowing softly.

"Say, Danbom," Chaplain Hallowell said, "there seems to be some confusion about where we're supposed to be during this deal. There's no Chaplain Section in a rifle company and Sergeant Jackson thinks we're supposed to be attached to the Battalion Aid Station."

"That's it according to the table of organization," I said.

"But that's with H and S and we're Virgins," Duff said.

"You're virgins. I'm a rabbi," Horowitz said.

"Big V, Virgins," Duff amended.

"A V is a V."

"I'll square it away with Jackson in the morning," I said.

I sat down on my bunk and studied the shoes on my feet. They were undistinguished boondockers as scuffed and worn and run-down as my soul. Chaplain Duff came and sat down beside me. "Have you called Ella?" he asked.

"Yes, sir," I said. "I called her yesterday."

"Miss Pollard tells us she's leaving for Orlando."

"Yes," I said, "she is."

"We're sorry to hear that, Danbom," Chaplain Hallowell said.

I didn't want them to be sorry. I was afraid I'd burst into tears if there was any more sorrow around me. "I told her the truth and she didn't believe me," I said.

"Oh, I see," Chaplain Duff said in a subdued tone which set my throat pumping. "Well, maybe she isn't the girl for you. Maybe this is His way of saving you from an error."

"His way!" I cried and I felt the blood flame in my face. "His way! Don't hand me that! Don't give me that Overseer stuff. She's there and she's real whether I'm looking at her or not and nobody's saving me from any error and if they are I want to make it. That's one error I want to make if it kills me. She loves me, Chaplain; Miss Pollard says so, but she doesn't believe me! She's willing to forgive me if I give up the Girl from Escondido, but to do that I have to lie to her and pretend that I can, but I can't because she never was!"

Chaplain Duff was taken aback. Hallowell and Horowitz crossed the hut to my side. "Calm down, Danbom," Hallowell said gently.

"Calm! How can I be calm? It's like Alice!"

"Who?" Horowitz asked.

"Through the looking glass."

"Look, Danbom," Horowitz said, "before you ring any more girls into this thing let me call Ella. I'll call her tomorrow."

"What'll you tell her that I haven't already?" I asked.

Horowitz thought extensively.

"Yes, what will you tell her?" Hallowell asked.

"Don't rush me," Horowitz said.

There was a prolonged silence filled with lucubration.

"What is, is," Horowitz said presently.

"In this case, Nathan, what is not, also is," Duff said.

Horowitz nodded. "I'll accept that," he said.

I fell back on my bunk. "Don't, please," I groaned. "Just let me suffer in my own way. Don't tangle me up anymore. Please don't."

They left me, but far into the night I heard them arguing in an amiable and earnest manner. Good and evil, positive and negative, Yin and Yang, absence and presence, being and non-being, all two sides of an indescribable coin. Their arguments escalated, switching back and forth up the mountainsides of theological philosophy leaving me stranded in the valley far below.

My poor brain ached. It quivered, floating in my skull like a weary jellyfish, trailing tendrils of hope and despair and never finding anything to which it could cling.

Somebody blew a whistle. I leaped up, probing my ear with one finger to extract the piercing sound as consciousness invaded my mind like a cold salt comber smashing across the beach.

"Let's go! Fall in! This is it!"

A sergeant flashed a light through our hut, then ran out slamming the door behind him. I snapped on the lights and saw the chaplains huddled in the aisle, their faces white with sleepiness and shock.

"Hey!" I said. "Let's go!"

We scrambled into our clothes and assembled our gear. My fingers fumbled my buttons and buckles. I was excited and so were the chaplains. We moved swiftly, quietly, each of us wrapped in concentrated haste and a sense of urgency.

War had come and all the contradictions and absurdities of life vanished. I felt alive and vital again, ready to march off whistling a martial air.

There was a purpose, a direction, goals and rewards.

War is a tonic, an elixir. It's better than Coca-Cola or hard spirits. The chaplains smiled and so did I. We were comrades in arms.

We hoisted the organ and went into the street. The men spilled out of their Quonset whales with packs and rifles and intent expressions on their unwashed faces. The sergeants trotted about bellowing good-naturedly as we fell into formation. It was past midnight, and the V's on our helmet liners glowed like fireflies, or dim miners' lanterns. Captain Crowell appeared, his helmet distinguished from ours by the two bars he'd run over and under the V to make it look like the Roman numeral $\overline{\underline{\text{V}}}$. Sergeant Jackson called for attention. Captain Crowell had a few words to say.

"Men," he said, "we've got a lot riding on the outcome of this show. It's not a big one but it's important and I want you all to remember that the brass is watching. As you know, we're out to demonstrate mobility on foot and to show the brass what foot-soldiering should be. This is a guerrilla action so I'm depending on every man in the company to show individual initiative. Man for man we're as good as any Marines alive. Now let's get out there and run rings around the Escondidos! And remember, men— V is for Victory!"

It was electrifying. Captain Crowell tapped the edge of his helmet in a gallant little salute, then he led out. The First Platoon followed him and presently the whole company was on the march, the phosphorescent V's on their helmet liners bobbing in the darkness.

The chaplains and I fell in at the tag end of the column and moved along to the sound of marching feet and the jingle of buckle and rifle.

The Escondidos were supposedly dug into the hills somewhere beyond Horno Ridge, but the only people who knew this for certain were the umpires whose duty it was to referee and control the maneuver. They wore white helmets and white armbands and had a special radio net to monitor the exercise.

A jeep, burning a green flare, loaded with colonels, bucked toward us over the rough ground. The color green was for observers.

Some of the umpires carried flags, yellow ones, red ones with white circles in the center, orange ones, black ones, each with a specific meaning according to the rules. Some were for artillery and mortar fire, others were used to mark the limits of advance.

There was an umpire for each platoon and so many for each company staff, they carried clipboards and casualty tags, pieces of cardboard with strings on them. Each tag had a picture of the injury the recipient was supposed to have suffered. For a broken leg, there was a picture of a broken leg, likewise for arms, necks and heads.

One tag simply had D.O.W. on it in large letters. It meant Dead of Wounds.

It was a dark, windless night with a dull moon. The men tramped along, hushed, rumpled, and eager. We trailed them contentedly and the field organ was strangely silent as though it too was awed by the imminence of battle.

Then Hallowell remembered that the question of our status had not yet been resolved.

Duff said he felt at home with the Virgins, but Horowitz thought we ought to play it kosher, find Jackson and get a decision.

The chaplains' packs were freighted with religious gear so I suggested they stay at the tail of the column while I went forward and conferred with Jackson. The chaplains agreed and as I left, the organ let off a prodigious squawk; Hallowell had stumbled on the rough ground and jarred the thing awake.

When I reached the head of the column, it was stalled. Men crouched in the ditch on either side of a road warned me to get down. "Escondidos!" they hissed.

The scouts had made contact with an Escondido outpost and Jackson had gone ahead to investigate.

Perhaps if I hadn't been on an independent mission I wouldn't have noticed the anxiety in their faces. They were crouched and tense; their heads slewed about at every rustling sound and their eyes probed the darkness, straining to clear an area of safety far beyond the limits of their vision. They were already deeply engaged in the show, but I was still detached.

Several of them who'd seen me take my pasting in the combat village asked how it felt to get hit by a blank. I was tempted to take mean advantage of my experience and say it just about killed me. I was sure some of them had taken a shot at me that day and in one real sense those blanks had killed me, but instead I relieved their apprehension. "If they don't break the skin the welts go away in a day or so," I said. "It's the muzzle blast that gets you."

They nodded, the Virgin V's on their helmets chopping up and down like arrowheads.

"Jackson been gone long?" I asked.

"About five minutes."

"I'll go after him."

"Take it easy, Danbom," one of the Virgins said.

They regarded me as a veteran.

I hadn't gone very far when my name was called.

"Danbom?"

I stopped but couldn't see anyone.

"Over here. It's me."

"Me who?"

"Jackson."

I groped toward the sound of Jackson's voice and found him by touch. He was dressed like a yucca with cactus spears sticking out of the net around his helmet. I pricked my finger and yelped.

"Pretty good, huh?" he said.

"Sharp," I said. "Who are you?"

"A skirmishing scout," Jackson said, "but with all this crap on I can't see anything."

I asked him where the Chaplain Section was supposed to be.

"I sent a man back to tell you," Jackson said.

"He didn't find us."

"You're supposed to connect up with the Battalion Medical Platoon after all."

"But that makes us Escondidos, doesn't it?"

"All I know is that you're supposed to be with Battalion Med."

"Where is it located?"

"You'll have to ask the first umpire you come to. Identify the chaplains and he'll tell them where to go. We're not supposed to know the disposition of H and S units."

"When did you send that man back?" I asked.

"About ten minutes ago."

"Oh, mother!"

When I got back to the tail of the column the chaplains were gone. One of the Virgins told me which umpire they'd been talking to and I asked him where Battalion Med was supposed to be. "Somewhere in San Onofre Canyon," he said, "but they aren't on the radio net yet, so I guess they're still moving. Your chaplains are headed over that way now. I told them to check with the next umpire they bumped into."

"What if they don't bump into one?" I asked.

"They've got a map and a compass," he said.

I took off at a trot in the direction the umpire had indicated, hoping the chaplains wouldn't use their compasses until I reached them. They'd be hard enough to find if they didn't know where they were going. If they thought they knew it could be impossible.

I jogtrotted until my wind gave out, then stopped to get my bearings. There were clouds licking the face of the moon and the landscape seemed to pitch and toss as the light played over it. To my left was a hill which would have blocked their progress. I held my breath, listening, thinking perhaps I'd passed them. I couldn't hear anything except wind in the mesquite. I moved on, sure now that I'd lost my chaplains who were wandering about like unbelled sheep.

The Lord is their shepherd, I thought. He'll make them to lie down in Battalion Med.

And suddenly it occurred to me that if this was so I was free. Me, Charlie Danbom, free as a bird, and Oceanside was only twenty miles away!

I was in no-man's land, somewhere between the Escondidos and the Virgins. I was detached—no one was watching me. The exercise was scheduled for two days. I could slip away, see Ella and maybe never be missed. The prospect took my breath away.

I turned and started toward the ocean, but I hadn't gone twenty paces when a mournful sound arrested me. It was the organ braying from the top of the hill. I could have killed it.

The sound died and I stood there torn between duty and love. "Goddamn it, Lord," I said, "you take them."

The organ brayed again, B flat.

They'd climbed the hill. Hill, hell, it was a precipice. I snapped a match and checked my field map. The area on top of the hill was clearly marked: Restricted. Out of bounds.

"Hath not a chaplain eyes?" I grumbled, but I remembered Horowitz going to the dance because he hadn't been invited.

San Onofre Canyon was on the other side of the hill and that's where they were headed. Naturally, Horowitz would insist on traversing a restricted area.

Obviously, the Lord had led His lost sheep astray. I got to the base of the hill and climbed; it was a scramble and should have been impossible for three men and an organ, but another bray authenticated their presence above. I reached the top and paused to catch my breath.

In the distance, far below, I could see headlights on Basilone Road. I thought of Ella, fast asleep, dreaming of Orlando, and it cut deep. I waited and another bray from the organ gave me the chaplains' azimuth. I headed toward the sound, but I hadn't gone twenty yards when my leg hit a wire.

I traced it to an iron stake with a flag on it, a red flag with a white square in the center. Mines.

"Hey, Chaplains," I yelled, "you're in a mine field!"

I waited, scared stiff, then Duff's voice carried back. "Whose field?" he called.

"A mine field!" I bellowed.

"An Italian truck farmer," Horowitz said.

"This is Danbom!" I yelled. "A mine field. Explosives!"

There was a profound silence.

I tried to guess the safety radii for the demolitions; usually each canister was taped off, but since the area had been marked out of bounds this precaution may have been thought unnecessary. It could be blank 105mm howitzer shells, M-80 firecrackers, simulated hand grenades, flares, or smoke pots. It could be anything. I didn't know. I stood at the stake with the wire in my hand knowing it could activate the whole field, or that the field might be timed to go off automatically. I heard the field organ sigh pathetically.

Most military exercises get "blooded" before they're over. Somebody breaks an arm, or drowns, or his parachute fails to open, or he steps on a simulated artillery shell. It's expected and usually charged off to statistics, the excuse being that out of the same number of men going about their normal business, one or two will have an automobile accident, or fall off a ladder, or get hit by a baseball. This argument never appealed to me and I didn't think it would hold if we lost three chaplains in the first night of a company maneuver. The National Council of Churches and similar bodies would no doubt send letters of protest. Their loss wouldn't go down like the fabled chaplains of three faiths who joined hands and sank with their ship in that long-ago war for freedom.

I told the chaplains to stay where they were and picked my way cautiously along the wire. For some reason I felt expendable. I had the feeling I'd seen the action in a movie and that I knew exactly what to do.

I heard them praying in three languages, English, Latin and Hebrew.

"Stand fast, men," I shouted and my voice had a heroic ring to it. "Keep calm."

Presently I saw three shaking V's glowing in the dark; then the chaplains were dimly outlined against the night sky—*veni, vidi, vici.* Horowitz and Duff were carrying the organ. Hallowell spotted my V and waved. "Over here, Danbom," he said tremulously.

I tried to remember the next line, or piece of business, from the guts and glory action movie which had supported me to this point, but I couldn't. My mind was blank and I experienced the actor's panic when he knows he's blown. My silver-screen courage vanished in the realization that we were in fact standing smack in the middle of the pyrotechnic display Colonel Pollard had devised to give verisimilitude to his maneuver. One false move and his fondest hopes would be realized.

"What'll we do, Danbom?" Horowitz asked.

Duff was praying quietly. "*Fratres: Si consurrexistus cum Christo: quae sursum sunt quaerite, ubi Christus est dextera Dei sedens: quae sursum sunt apite, non quae super terram.*"

The wire I had followed was still clutched in my hand. It was filled with high-voltage terror and I couldn't let it go. "Retrace your steps," I whispered shakily. Then, struck by the good sense this represented, I said it again so they could hear me. "Retrace your steps. You got in this far; we should be able to get out the same way."

They came toward me, moving gingerly, Hallowell first, probing the ground with his toe before he put his foot down, Horowitz and Duff following in his steps.

"Straight on," I whispered. "Go lightly. Follow the wire."

"What wire?" Horowitz asked.

"Right here," Duff whispered.

Chaplain Hallowell reached my side and smiled nervously. "Glad to see you, Danbom," he said.

Horowitz and Duff were just behind him. Horowitz wiped his brow with one hand and sighed. "Let's rest this thing," he said to Duff.

I noticed, too late, that Duff was on one side of the wire, Horowitz on the other. I tried to warn them, but as they lowered the organ on the wire, it snapped. My jaw locked full open. I tried to speak, but couldn't. I ran.

The chaplains came with me.

We reached the crest of the hill and as we dove for

cover a massive explosion shook the ground and the air was filled with B flat.

In the red flash which lit the sky I saw the field organ rise straight up, turning end over end. Its anguished bray changed to a discordant shriek as it began its descent, and air streaming through its exposed bellows gave off a chord like the sound of a great Amen.

Chaplain Duff's face was stone white. He crouched trembling beside us, looking out across that field.

The shattered organ lay groaning piteously as multicolored flares shot aloft, illuminating the area in garish light.

Duff started over the top but Hallowell grabbed him. "I can't leave it out there!" Duff cried.

"You'll get blown up."

Then to my astonishment Horowitz scrambled over the top and ran toward the organ, flattening each time another flare went off.

"Horowitz!" Duff yelled. He tore himself from Hallowell's grasp and ran. "Nathan, come back!"

Chaplain Horowitz had almost reached the organ when Duff tackled him. They rolled over, struggling.

"Don't be a damned fool, Nathan!"

"I cared about that organ as much as you did."

"You're a *tsaddik* and a *shmendrik*," I heard Duff say.

"And you're a *schlemiel*," Horowitz replied.

With flares, rockets and the explosions all around, Chaplains Duff and Horowitz sat out there smiling at each other as the little four-octave Estey field organ died.

I felt a pang of remorse because I'd wished the organ gone and now it was, but I was glad it wasn't me lying there with my bellows, pipes and keys exposed to the sky.

Above us the flares spat and glittered trailing smoke as they descended on their chutes. Horowitz and Duff crept back.

"Come on," I said. "We'll circle the hill and locate Battalion Med."

Duff glanced back at the organ and for a moment I thought he was going to take out his kit and administer the last rites, but he just shook his head sadly and we went down the hill.

"War is hell on organs," Horowitz said.

A gray streak of light appeared on the horizon as we pushed through the underbrush. Off to our left a howitzer barked, one round for effect, then it was silent. We reached the mouth of San Onofre Canyon and headed in to connect with Battalion Med.

I found the road and we plodded along quietly, letting the raw edge of our recent experience heal over. I sorted through the sensations which had gripped me, the jumping back and forth between the false and real.

In the presence of genuine danger I'd resorted to playing a part and it scared me to think how easily a man could get killed that way. I decided that in a real battle each man must believe that the enemy is shooting blanks. If he couldn't do that he'd dig in and stay down. And I concluded that heroism was a kind of reverse twist on clapping for Tinker Bell.

I wondered if the artillery was firing support for our maneuver, or running one of their own. Usually there were three or four tactical exercises going at once with men mushing around in the boondocks attacking, defending, charging the beaches, or dropping out of the sky. When you came right down to it, Camp Pendleton was one big guts and glory action fiction factory.

"We want to thank you for pulling us out of that mess back there," Horowitz said.

"Don't thank me, thank the organ. If I hadn't heard it I'd be long gone by now."

"Long gone where?" Hallowell asked.

"Long gone to Oceanside," I said and I stopped walking. "Now listen, you just stay on this road and you're bound to run into Battalion Med. If I don't get to Ella, all I'll ever be is a brig and battle rat. I'd turned you over to the hands of God, but He goofed, as you can see."

"The hands of Who?" Hallowell asked.

"Now wait a minute," I said.

"I thought you were a declines-to-state," Duff said.

"I believe in the compass and field map. I'm going to Oceanside before Ella goes to Orlando and before I get tangled up in this thing again."

"Hold up a minute," Hallowell said. "That's desertion in the face of the enemy, isn't it?"

"It's pretend desertion in the face of a pretend enemy and they can pretend shoot me for it!" I said. "They can pretend bury me and you can pretend pray over me, but I'm going to Ella."

"They'll court-martial you again," Horowitz said.

"Absent without leave is all they can nail me with. If I make it off the base I can be in Oceanside before noon."

"And if you don't make it off the base?" Duff asked.

"I'll have tried."

"You'd have had a better chance last night in the dark," Hallowell said, "but you came back for us."

"Duty called," I said.

"In the voice of an organ?" Duff asked. "But, Danbom, how do you know that this wasn't—"

"Stop!" I cried. "Don't tell me that He spake from the organ—from mountaintops and burning bushes, all right —but not from that portable organ. Look, you were in trouble. I came to help. I'm strictly humanist, see? That's all there was to it. Now you'd better get linked up and start working out an alibi before Colonel Pollard starts wondering who blew up his simulators."

I walked across the field to a gully that ran along the road where I could make my way back without being seen. I dropped down the embankment and started away, but the chaplains dropped in after me.

I turned on them angrily. "Come on now, shove off! I don't want your company. Go mesh with the military, that's what you're here for."

"Danbom," Horowitz said, "we'd like to help you."

"Don't help me!" I pleaded. "I've had all the help from you I can stand. You're in the show here; play your parts. I'm copping out. I invented one girl, one lousy, little, imaginary girl and she squeezed all the pretend right out of me. I can't play anymore, but you go right ahead. Join Pollard's war. The pretend casualties will be coming in soon and they'll need your pretend consolation. The only anchor I've got in this crazy world is Ella, so I've got to go."

I turned and trotted down the gully, smashing through the mesquite growing out of the sandy bottom. I was in a hurry to get away before the umpires started moving around.

I glanced over my shoulder once and saw the chaplains still in the gully, then I rounded a bend and put on a burst of speed to lose them as fast as possible.

After a few minutes I stopped and looked for a place to stash my pack and helmet where I could find them in case I made it back to the base without getting caught. I was just twisting out of my pack straps when I heard a sound ahead. I dropped behind some brush and saw an Escondido mortar platoon. They were coming straight for me.

The Escondidos wore caps. The mortar tubes, base plates and shells looked dreadfully lethal. The man on the point walked along, rifle ready, his eyes scanning the bank on either side. His mouth was a tense, lipless slit and his eyes were those of a bitter marksman. A rifle team followed on his heels, each man walking half crouched, their footsteps springy and silent in the loose sand.

I said to myself it's a game. They're pretending. It isn't real. Ella is waiting; duck around them. Let them pass, skip out. But the back of my neck was cold and the palms of my hands were wet.

I licked my dry lips and scuttled back on my belly, looking for better cover. Every furtive move I made increased my apprehension. It's physiological, I said to myself, the symptoms will pass. But they didn't. My scalp tingled exactly as it had when I was a kid playing hide and go seek at Interdom—that delicious sensation of fear and triumph which comes when the guy who's looking for you stops so close that you could touch him.

I could see the Escondidos, but they hadn't yet seen me.

I was superior, smarter, the observer unobserved, but I knew that in a few more seconds the man on the point would stumble into me and I'd be jerked, full born, out of nothingness into their consciousness with no appeal and no way back.

Again I counseled myself not to play, to give it up, but the man on the point was bearing down. I thought of the chaplains back in the gully. They too were, as yet, nothing to the Escondidos, but I knew they were there and I had to save them if I could.

The man on the point was five yards away when I broke cover and ran like a hysterical rabbit back down the gully. As I rounded the bend a shot was fired and I heard the Escondidos yell, "We got you, Virgin!"

"Missed me!" I hollered and I ran back into the illusion. When I reached the chaplains I was waving my arms frantically and yelling for them to run too. "Escondidos!" I howled. "A whole platoon! Run!"

Chaplain Hallowell caught my arm. "Wait a minute, Danbom," he said calmly. "We've been talking this over."

"Goddamn it!" I yelled. "They're in the gully."

"They aren't Escondidos," Duff said rationally.

"Don't tell me they aren't! I know Escondidos when I see them. They're wearing caps. Hightail it!"

"Danbom," Horowitz said, "forget this *meshugah* war game. Go on. Head for Oceanside." He pushed me back in the direction I'd come.

I resisted fiercely. "You're pushing me into the enemy," I cried.

"Aren't we on their side?" Hallowell asked.

"I don't know!"

"Use your head," Horowitz said. "It's a game."

"I tell you they're there!"

At that moment the Escondidos appeared, running toward us. "Give up!" they yelled.

I saw the transformation in the chaplains' faces. Their reason was swept away. A brief, wide-eyed, slack-jawed blankness was followed by astonishment, then the dark hue of panic flooded their eyes and we scrambled up the bank leaving divots of earth behind our digging feet.

The Escondidos fired at us. "Come on, we got you!" one of them yelled.

Ignoring their outraged cries that we were dead, we ran over the field to the road, our slapping feet raising clouds of dust. The road turned and I saw the Battalion Field Hospital located under a pram tent about fifty yards ahead. We raced toward it, Hallowell chuffing like a one-cylinder engine, Duff's plump figure concentrated into a ball with arms and legs, and Horowitz galloping like a camel. The corpsmen who had been idling about the tent leaped up and snatched their weapons. "Hold your fire!" I yelled.

"Virgins!" the corpsmen cried and throwing themselves down on their bellies they opened fire.

We dove into the ditch. "We're noncombatants!" Horowitz yelled, but his protest was lost in gunfire.

We lay pressed to the ground. The Escondidos who had been chasing us, hearing the rapid fire from the corpsmen, hit the deck and answered it. We were caught in the crossfire between the corpsmen and the Escondidos.

"They're on the same side, aren't they?" Hallowell asked.

I nodded. "But they don't know it yet."

"They shouldn't attack a hospital!" Horowitz declared. "That's barbarian! Don't they see the red cross?"

"They must think the Virgins captured it."

"The Virgins wouldn't do a thing like that," Duff said.

I poked my head up and saw two Navy doctors run out of the hospital tent followed by an umpire. "What's going on!" one doctor yelled.

"Virgins!"

"Cease fire," the doctor yelled and he began waving his arms.

We took advantage of the confusion and sprinted toward the hospital tent taking fire from both sides.

The H and S Company Fat Wagon with Sergeant Strand at the wheel careened down the road and slewed to a stop, throwing a screen of dust over the area.

When it settled, Colonel Pollard was there, his swagger stick thrashing and his face tight as the Turk's head knot on its handle. "Who ordered this firing?" he demanded.

The Escondido mortarmen stood up and crossed the road.

"Those men opened up on the Aid Station, sir," one of the doctors said.

"That's fat!" Pollard swore.

"There's a couple platoons of Virgins loose around here," one of the mortarmen said.

"Where?" Pollard demanded.

"There's four of them," the mortarman said and he pointed us out.

Colonel Pollard swung around. He saw the chaplains and his face bleached white. The swagger stick in his hand quivered and he began flagellating his leg. *Swip, swop, swop, swip.*

"Sir," I said, "Captain Crowell said the chaplains were to be attached to Battalion Med for the exercise."

Swip, swop, swip.

"We had a little trouble getting linked up," Hallowell said.

Swop, swop.

"Lost the organ," Duff said.

From snowy white, Pollard's face flushed purple. The swagger stick whistled as he struck himself.

"Fortunes of war," Horowitz said.

An umpire, who had been figuring on his clipboard with fateful intensity, finished his calculations and approached the colonel. "Casualty assessment, sir," he said.

"What's that?" Pollard demanded.

"Casualty assessment, sir. Five men dead, seven wounded. Twelve, total."

"What!" Pollard cried. "These are my men. They're Escondidos!"

"Twelve, sir," the umpire said.

"But that's ridiculous!"

The umpire didn't look up. He began separating casualty tags from a pack in his hand. "Twelve, sir," he said again. "This was the first contact; the surprise was total and the attack came on your rear, which doubles the effect of the fire. The fact that the men were firing at their own units doesn't negate the rules, sir. Would you care to check my figures?"

Swop!

Pollard shook his head. "All right," he said. He raised his swagger stick and his eyes spat death. "Kill that one," he said, pointing at Hallowell, "and that one," pointing at Horowitz, "and that one," he said, pointing at Duff, "and kill that one," pointing at me.

It was an act of murder, pure and simple, and the pleasure of committing it glittered in the colonel's eyes.

"But sir, by their helmets they're Virgins," the umpire said.

"No, they're Escondidos," Pollard said. "Dead Escondidos."

"Three Chaplains killed in one engagement? Isn't that a bit unusual?"

"Not in my outfit it isn't," Pollard said and he grinned icily. "Go on tag them."

The umpire handed each of us a tag and told us to fasten them to our blouses. The tags read D.O.W.—dead of wounds.

The colonel watched as we tied the tags in our buttonholes and kept flailing himself with the swagger stick until I couldn't help but see that ritual murder was infinitely more satisfactory than any other kind. One is able to prolong and savor it without guilt or fear of retribution. There's no problem about disposing of a lumpy, inert body and the terror of extinction doesn't die with the victim, it lingers.

We did not take death calmly. Our fingers fumbled as we affixed the fatal tags and the colonel beat his leg. *Swop, swip! Swip, swop!* He studied our eyes for hidden changes there and must have been satisfied because he marched back to the Fat Wagon, refreshed and tipped Strand a jaunty salute. As he boarded the wagon I noticed a trickle of blood running down his sock into his shoe.

To the colonel we were as dead as doornails, mackerel and yesterday's news.

We looked at each other seeking assurance of our existence in each other's eyes, then Hallowell sighed. "If this is heaven, I'm disappointed," he said. "Or maybe I went the other way."

"Come on, let's get inside before we begin to stink up the place," Horowitz said and he shoved us toward the hospital tent.

Ten

THE Base medical staff was playing a game too. Dead and wounded from our exercise were to be evacuated to a collection and clearing company and given mock treatment for their mock wounds, after which they would lay over for a number of hours, depending on the nature of their injury, before being fed back into battle. According to these rules a dead man was out of action for twelve hours, which the chaplains and I thought was a generous allowance.

Being dead, we were more or less in the way. The corpsmen and doctors ignored us pointedly, making us feel that we were something of a sanitation problem, but we didn't know how to inter ourselves. Let the dead past bury the dead may be good advice, but it's difficult to put into practice.

I hoped that an ambulance or a hearse would take us back to base where, if luck would have it, I could skin out for

Oceanside. I didn't think they'd miss a corpse, unless they were running classes in mock embalming. But as the afternoon wore on and no one came to dispose of us I began once more to despair.

The two doctors were Navy commanders on reserve duty. Doc Pickering was a tall, misty-eyed obstetrician from Berkeley, California; Doc Katz, a dark, cynical-looking ophthalmologist from St. Louis. When the first casualties started coming in, Katz told Pickering to handle the Virgins. "It'll broaden your experience, Pickering," he said.

Pickering snorted bitterly and went to work instructing the corpsmen in first aid and evacuation procedure. The casualties were treated for abdominal wounds, head wounds, broken limbs, burns and what not, then put into ambulances and consigned to base.

As a rule the casualties relaxed and enjoyed it, but occasionally a man would be so deep in the hypnotic influence of the war game that he would beg someone to write his mother, or his girl. If the chaplains hadn't been dead they could have helped such cases; they discussed doing so anyway, but they weren't awfully sure that these boys weren't trying to pull someone's leg.

There was simply no way for us to know. It was hot and we were tired. The ambulances coming and going raised clouds of dust which never quite settled; the outlines of objective reality were obscured and we'd run out of tools to test it. The doctors had thermometers and stethoscopes and when a man came in suffering from real heat prostration they could tell. They could distinguish real bruises and cuts and sprains from the fake ones, but we'd given up long ago.

A couple of dead Escondidos and a few dead Virgins joined us in our corner of the tent. They'd shed their enmity after having crossed the river Styx on the D.O.W. One of the Escondidos produced a pack of cards and they began playing poker for heavy stakes payable upon resurrection and complaining because the casualties were being taken right back to base while the dead had to wait.

They gave us a sketchy account of what was happening at the front. The Escondidos were on the move and the Virgins were retiring.

"As they should be," Duff said, but his smile got no response.

About four o'clock in the afternoon a hitch developed in the evacuation procedure. The ambulances stopped coming and the aid station began to fill up. Doc Pickering called the Base to find out what was wrong, but couldn't get any satisfaction so he joined a poker game with the dead, but he had to pay cash to play.

Some time later, two wounded Virgins were brought in on stretchers and the Escondido casualties set up a howl.

"Cut hell out of them, Doc."

"Give them fats the knife!"

The Virgins were actually nervous. One of them had a splinted leg and the other had his arm in a sling. They rolled their eyes and tried to communicate with each other without speaking in the presence of their foes. Chaplain Duff asked me to comfort them.

"I'm just as dead as you are," I said. "What can *I* do?"

"Tell them they're protected by the Geneva Convention and give them these." Duff rustled in his pack and brought out a couple of missals.

To my surprise these were gratefully received. The Virgins thanked me. They were a part of a weapons platoon that had been cut off and surrounded. The younger, fatter one started to tell me more, but the other silenced him. "Interrogation officer," he said.

"I'm just a dead Marine," I said.

"Disguised interrogation officer," the Virgin said. "Name, rank and serial number—that's all we're supposed to say. And don't eat nothing either because they've got truth syrup."

"We don't have any truth syrup," I said, but the Virgins wouldn't talk to me anymore. They put aside the stuff I'd given them and lay with their mouths clamped shut, staring at the canvas roof.

There was a vacant litter at the back of the tent. I stretched out on it, folded my hands across my chest, and closed my eyes. I was on a bier, bloodless and waxy with my eyes and mouth sewn shut. There were voices, hushed and mournful, organ music and the scent of too many flowers. He died a virgin, they said, cut down before he could reach his prime. There's those as say he was killed on purpose, sacrificed like a lamb, poor boy.

They filed past, all of them, and pecked my marble forehead, leaving now and then a tear or two.

It's the likes of him as keeps our country strong and free, they said.

Weller came and looked and couldn't believe I was dead. Laperuta, Powell and Morgan were afraid.

Go on, boys, have a last look at your comrade.

No, some other time, perhaps.

They hoisted me up and paraded me down the street. I

was in the obituary column, but not the telephone book. I was begat, but forever unbegetting. They lowered me and the sun went down.

When the first clod of earth hit my shoulder I sat up with a yawp. "Wait!"

Chaplain Duff was at my side. It was dark. He shook my shoulder gently. "It's me, Danbom," he said.

"Didn't Ella even come?" I asked.

"Wake up, boy," he said.

I looked around wild-eyed. The tent was illuminated by a single Coleman lantern. Most of the casualties were asleep on their stretchers. Rain was falling with a sound like a drummer's brush and Pickering and Katz were playing chess.

"Man," I said, "I thought I was dead."

"You are," Duff said.

"That's right. What time is it?"

"Close to midnight."

Chaplains Hallowell and Horowitz joined Duff. They had their ponchos on and they squatted down for all the world like witches. "Let's go," Horowitz whispered.

"Where?" I asked.

"We're taking you to Oceanside," Hallowell said.

An ambulance arrived, its wheels churning mud as it shuddered up the grade to the tent. The casualties sat up and began clamoring to be taken back to the base. Pickering and Katz had already decided that it was stupid to waste ambulance space on the dead, but now they had to adjudicate the dispute between the abdominal wounds and the head wounds as to which had priority on the transportation.

The head wounds threw fits and the abdominal wounds

groaned piteously, pleading to be put out of their misery.

"Now's the time," Duff said. "Let's beat it."

"You don't have to come," I said. "You'll only get in trouble and slow me up."

"I'm going to call Miss Pollard," Hallowell said. "I think she'd drive us down to Oceanside and back. At least she'll call Ella and let her know you're coming."

Pickering and Katz were yelling at the head wounds who were forcing their way into the ambulance. A couple of blows were struck and the corpsmen waded in to separate the wounded men. Katz threatened to kill them if they didn't straighten up.

"I'm catching cold," a head wound complained.

"You'll catch a bloody goddamned clout on the head if you don't get out of the driver's seat."

The dead Virgins and Escondidos watched this argument with Olympian detachment, then lay down and went back to sleep.

Duff tugged my arm. "Come on," he said, "faint heart never won fair lady."

I gathered my gear, put my poncho on and as the doctors and corpsmen restored order among the casualties, the chaplains and I ducked under the tent flap and slipped away into the night.

A pock-faced moon showed occasionally through the sculling clouds and a salt wind off the ocean stirred the grass as we moved furtively toward the gully, stopping like thieves at every rustling sound. We grouped ourselves like stalking Africans, our faces tense as hunters. We signaled and cautioned each other with signs so old, so instinctive, that no one had to check a manual to see what was meant. Finger to lips for silence. Hand palm out, for Halt, I hear something! Point, for direction. Nod, for go ahead.

All over the hills if men were moving at all they were skulking. They were skulking because we were skulking and we were skulking because they were skulking. Skulking is contagious.

"*Sha!*" Horowitz said. We stopped, poised. We listened.

It was the ambulance. The abdominal wounds had won priority and were cheering as they rode away and the head wounds were cursing them.

We moved on, reached the gully and crouched on our haunches like Bushmen.

"Pickets may be out," Duff whispered. "Keep low."

We slipped along the muddy gully floor cautiously, flattening at every sound. Hallowell thought we ought to camouflage ourselves and smeared his face with mud.

It helped.

When we were well beyond the Med Station area, I trotted ahead to where our gully debouched into a field. Off to the left I saw lights on Basilone Road. The chaplains joined me, their eyes focused distrustfully on the alien road where the white man devil cars were passing.

"Basilone Road," I whispered. "Five miles cross-country to U.S. 101. Fifteen to Oceanside."

"Telephone?" Chaplain Hallowell asked, making a dialing sign.

"Camp Horno," I whispered. "Booth there."

Hallowell nodded. "Brandy," he said.

We ran forward and flopped on our bellies beside the

road where we took the camp under surveillance. There was a telephone booth about fifty yards away, one of those all-glass, aluminum jobs, standing near a parking lot.

"All right," I whispered, "into the parking lot and hit the deck."

We waited as a car passed, then we ran like flushed deer and fell in a heap in the lot and waited for the crickets to signal the all-clear.

"From here on it's nerve," I said.

"*Chutzpe*," Horowitz said.

"You and I walk to the booth like we belonged," I whispered to Hallowell. We rose and started toward the booth.

"I can't remember her number," Hallowell whispered urgently before we'd gone four steps.

"Ask the operator," I said.

"I don't have any change."

I felt in my pockets. Nothing. Not one thin dime. "Duff!" I hissed into the darkness. "You got a dime, sir?"

Duff's head grew out of the hood ornament of an old Pontiac. He began fumbling through his pockets. "Call her collect," he said.

"Need a dime to get the operator," Hallowell said.

"I've got one," Duff yelped.

He thrust the dime at me. It felt funny. There was a hole in it.

Duff took the dime back, held it up to the sky and squinted, waiting for the moon. "St. Christopher medal," he said at last. "I didn't think I had a dime."

"Try it," Horowitz said.

Duff handed the medal to Hallowell. "It's about the size of a dime," he said.

"Is it honest?"

"With a war on he's arguing a dime's worth of morality? Try it," Horowitz insisted.

Caution forgotten we gathered around the phone booth. Hallowell went inside; he shut the door and the booth light flashed on. I kicked the door open. "No light," I said.

Hallowell inserted the medal in the coin slot. It ran through and dropped in the coin return box. We moaned. Hallowell fished the medal out. "Wrong slot, that was quarters," he whispered, "it's dark in here." He reinserted the coin in the dime slot; we stopped breathing. "I got a dial tone," he said excitedly.

"Get the operator. Quick."

Hallowell dialed. He got the operator.

"Operator?" he said. "Hello, operator?" He nodded to us. "Miss, I'd like to explain about the St. Christopher medal. Believe me it's not our intention to cheat your company, but you see there are four of us here . . . What's that? M-E-D-A-L. Yes, that's right. Medal." We waited, then Hallowell shook his head irritably. "Of course there's no St. Christopher medal listed," he said. "I put the medal in the coin slot."

"Forget the medal," I said, "tell her to call Miss Pollard, collect. Tell her it's your last medal."

"It's my last medal, operator," Hallowell said. "I'll send you a check. Could you please connect me with the home of Colonel Haskell Pollard?"

Hallowell turned to us, his face gray. "This isn't the base operator," he said.

"Tell her it's not a base medal," Duff cried.

"Tell her to connect you with the base operator."

"She wants to know what the St. Christopher medal was worth," Hallowell said.

"*Hock nischt kain cheinik!*" Horowitz cried. "Get the right operator."

"Yes, operator, the Patron Saint of Wayfarers," Hallowell said.

"Ferrymen, actually," Chaplain Duff said.

Horowitz waved his arms and rolled his eyes heavenward. "Tell her it's a plot to undermine the A. T. and T., but tell her to get your number."

"She has it," Hallowell cried.

A car swung into the parking lot, its lights caught us and we froze like cast figures on Mount Suribachi. As it turned into a parking space Duff, Horowitz and I vanished, leaving Hallowell in the booth. I scuttled under a car and lay with my face in the gravel. Two Marines got out and walked up the path to the camp. I waited until they'd gone, then I rolled out and stood up cautiously.

The phone booth was empty; the receiver dangled on the end of the cord.

I sprinted to the booth and caught the receiver.

"Hello."

"Freddie?—Where did you go?"

"Miss Pollard, this is Charles Danbom."

"I was just talking to Chaplain Hallowell," she said.

"Hold on." I searched the darkness and spotted Hallowell seated behind the wheel of a parked car. He got out, shut the door quietly and came to the booth shamefaced. "Hopped into the car," he said. "Two Marines went right past me."

I handed him the receiver. "She's still on," I said.

"Good thinking."

Chaplains Horowitz and Duff slid out from under the cars they'd picked for cover. Duff wiped his greasy hands on his dungarees and shook his head wearily. "Any casualties?" he asked.

"He's dead," I heard Hallowell say. "I know you just talked to him. I'm dead too. We're all dead. Your father killed us. Yes, of course you can."

Hallowell came out of the booth. "She wants to talk to you again," he said.

"Are you dead, Charlie?" Miss Pollard asked and she began to giggle. "Wass you dere, Charlie?" she asked.

"The colonel wiped us out, ma'am," I said.

"I guessed as much. What are you up to?"

"Going to Oceanside," I said.

"Greater love hath no man than that he should give up his life for a friend," Miss Pollard said. "Where are you now?"

"Camp Horno," I said.

"You've got a long way to go. How do you plan to get off the base? They'll stop you at the gate."

"We'll cut cross-country."

"All right, I'll call Ella. Do you know where Horno Canyon cuts into the Pacific Coast Highway?"

"I think so."

"I'll meet you there and drive you down."

"Thanks, ma'am," I said. "It may take us an hour or so. It's starting to rain harder."

"I'll wait," she said. "How's the exercise going?"

"I can't tell," I said.

"Dead men tell no tales, that it?"

"No, ma'am. I really don't know."

"All right, get going. When I tell Ella you're D.O.W. she's sure to wish she'd never let you go."

"Don't tell her that, ma'am. I'm not really D.O.W."

"It's as real as the Girl from Escondido, isn't it?" Miss Pollard asked and she hung up.

As I stepped out of the booth a coin dropped into the return box. I fingered it out and gave it to Duff. "The operator returned your St. Christopher medal," I said.

Duff smiled. "Bread upon the waters," he said, but he looked at the medal and frowned. "Wait, this isn't my medal. It's a dime."

"Transubstantiation," Horowitz said.

It was raining heavily now and the water coming down in sheets drummed on our helmet liners. I got my bearings and headed west toward the coast.

"It's nice of Miss Pollard to come out in this weather to drive us down," I said.

"Yes, it is indeed," Chaplain Duff said. "I doubt she'd have done it for anyone but Freddie."

"She's engaged," Hallowell said.

We splashed into a puddle and the water came over our boot tops.

"The tactical situation is fluid," Duff said. "Where are we?"

We were at the top of Horno Canyon which fell away five miles to the highway, but the rain had turned it into a cataract. "We'd better stick to the hills," I said. "A flash flood could wipe us out."

"Have you any idea yet what you're going to say to Ella?" Hallowell asked.

"No," I said, "I haven't."

"Remains to be seen," Horowitz said.

We climbed out of the canyon and hiked along the slippery ridge with the rain driving into our faces and running cold down the backs of our necks. Our packs soaked up water and doubled in weight, and our feet were like plumbers' helpers sucking mud with each step.

For half an hour we moved west. We crept up hills and shussed down to land in a heap, tangled, muddy and miserable. Tempers grew short but the chaplains kept themselves under control.

"Will you kindly remove that big, muddy, rabbinical boot from my face, Chaplain Horowitz?"

"Certainly, Chaplain Hallowell, if you can wait until brother Duff hoists himself off my back."

"If our military adviser will lend me a hand I'm sure we'll be on our feet again."

I pulled Duff up and helped the other two. They thanked me. They thanked each other.

"Adversity is the mother of courtesy," Duff said.

I'd been listening to the crump and whumple of artillery fire filtered by the rain, trying to guess which way the war had shifted, but the sound didn't tell me anything.

"Maybe they called it because of rain," Hallowell suggested.

Duff shook his head. "If they did that the rainmakers would rule the world," he said.

Horowitz sneezed violently. "Wonder if they'll give cold shots to a corpse?" he asked.

"Try Christian Science," Hallowell said.

Ordinarily this would have brought sparks to Horowitz' eyes, but the rain had damped his fires.

We pulled ourselves up another hill, suffering abrupt reversals when bushes we'd relied on for handholds tore out of the soggy earth and dumped us back. At the crest of the next ridge we found a mud road and splashed along it until Hallowell spotted a light and stopped. "A light!" he said.

"Hidden under a bushel," Duff said.

"A tent," Horowitz said.

We approached cautiously. There were several vehicles hub deep in mud near the tent; one of them had a limp two-star flag on the bumper. There was a radio jeep near the door and an umpire went into the tent carrying a message.

I signaled the chaplains to take cover and scuttled around to the rear where I could see into the tent through the lacings at the corner.

Inside, half a dozen officers were gathered around a plot board. Our Division C.O., General Wienkler, a big, gray-haired, genial man, was seated in a campaign chair next to a chilly-looking vice-admiral. A colonel handed General Wienkler a message. He scanned it, nodded and handed it back.

"They still chasing?" the admiral asked.

"Like a dog after its own tail. I know Pollard and he won't let go. He'll circle the Virgins until they're dizzy, then pounce." The general made a chopping gesture with his hand. "Pollard is a good man," he said, "eccentric in some respects, but a fine Marine."

The admiral picked up a mug of coffee from beside his chair and sipped it.

"Phase lines look like a basket of pretzels," the general said.

"Bad weather for an exercise," the admiral said.

"Soggy pretzels," the general said, "soggy pretzels."

"Hell," the admiral said, "I remember Pollard during the Inchon landing. He's efficient as scales on a snake. The way he moved troops off the beach was something to behold. Had it timed down to a gnat's eyelash. Didn't miss the schedule by sweat on a monkey's nuts."

The general nodded soberly. "He's a great organization man, great executive officer. Only problem is that he's a nit picker. Yes, sir, a nit picker and you can't put nit pickers in command position."

The admiral nodded gravely. "Same at sea," he said, "same at sea. You don't fish for smelt when there's whales around the corner."

The general wagged his head agreeably. "But they're still moving. That's one thing I'll hand Pollard. His people are moving and we can't even get down off this hill, unless we walk."

"This keeps up and we'll be able to sail," the admiral said.

I went back for the chaplains and found them huddled in the back seat of the general's command car. "Let's go," I said.

"The spirit is willing, but the flesh is wet," Hallowell said.

"It's only a couple of miles now. The war's still on, so we can make it. And Miss Pollard is waiting."

"That's right," Hallowell said, and the chaplains hopped out of the car and followed me.

The road dipped down the face of the ridge and we negotiated the drop on our backsides.

At the bottom we stood up and faced another climb. It took the starch out of us. We could hear water running in the canyon off to our left and started moving again when a challenge sent us rolling into the brush.

"Who goes there!"

It was a significant question. We looked into each other's muddy faces, wondering. "Tell him it's four dead men: a Protestant, a Catholic, a Jew and one declines-to-state," Horowitz said. "Makes quite a little shock force when you add it up."

I couldn't see the sentry, but he challenged again. It sounded like Weller.

"Hey, Weller, is that you?" I called.

"Who goes there?"

"Danbom!"

"Give me the password, Danbom, you creep!"

It was Weller. I stood up. "I forgot it, Weller," I called.

"Horse hockey."

"Okay," I said, "horse hockey. Who thought that one up?"

"That ain't it," Weller said. "You're a Virgin."

"So was your old man," I replied.

"Okay, wise guy," Weller called. "We'll get you!" He yelled for the corporal of the guard.

We ran.

Behind us there was the clatter of small arms fire and shouting. We splashed down behind some rocks and Hallowell rolled over on his back, half submerged. "Ah, to hell with it," he said. "A real war couldn't be worse."

A series of flares shot out from the crest of the hill, illuminating the canyon for a hundred yards. There was about three feet of water in it. If we'd had a rubber raft we could have reached the highway in about three minutes.

The small arms fire increased, mixed with the wet crush of simulated grenades. Smoke drifted toward us and a couple of umpires ran by waving red flares like votive candles. "Limit of advance," they yelled. "Limit of advance."

From down the hill across the creek other umpires with flares came toward us. "Limit of advance," they answered.

Overhead the flares burned out leaving us in the dark, but the noise of battle, clash and curse increased.

"Those are Virgin troops," I said. "They're attacking the Escondidos."

"Which is which?" Duff asked.

"I don't know."

Another flare splashed the sky illuminating two squads in the middle of the creek, waist-high in water. They yelled and flailed at each other with fists and rifles. "Virgins!" they yelled. "Escondidos!"

Umpires from both sides waded out to break up the melee. "Break it up! No body contact. You men are beyond the line of advance!"

The flares guttered out and the umpires were dumped into the water. There were howls of outrage, more running feet. "You're under arrest!"

"Arrest your Aunt Fanny," a Marine yelled.

A red flare floated past us, spluttering on the surface of the muddy water. An umpire rose under it and staggered to the bank. "Limit of advance," he gagged.

The dark was spiced with muzzle blast from M1 rifles, then the sounds diminished as the action moved away.

I heard Sergeant Strand bellowing and rose to my knees to locate him. His voice smashed along the creek, stirring the water. "Let's go, Escondidos! We've got 'em!"

A platoon of men ran down the hill, howling gloriously. They ran past us with their rifles at port, splashed through the water and vanished as the flare died overhead.

"Virgins?" Hallowell asked.

"Who knows?" I asked. "I didn't see their headgear."

"Caps, I think," Horowitz said.

"Escondidos, then," Duff said.

It grew quiet again. For a long time we sat in the mud with the rain beating on our backs. Our boots were full of water and we were chilled to the bone.

The dead-tag on my dungaree blouse was soggy; I tore it off, wadded it into a ball of pulp and flipped it away. I stood up, my boots whimpering as the water spurted out between the laces. I looked at the rain-pocked surface of the creek. For twenty cents I'd have pitched myself in the water and drowned.

Chaplain Hallowell sneezed mightily. "One more river to cross," he said.

I looked back at the triad huddled in the brush.

"Let's move out," Duff said, "over the hill to Oceanside, to Ella's house we go."

They were a pitifully sad, bedraggled sight. "Listen," I said, "I'll go on from here alone. Why don't you get out of this?"

Horowitz looked up at me and rain dripped off his helmet and ran down his long face. He smiled. "Danbom," he said, "do you know what lies over that hill?"

"The highway to Oceanside, I hope."

"And what is that?" Horowitz asked.

"It's a highway," I said.

"That highway is the road to reality," Horowitz said.

"What is God, Danbom?" Duff asked abruptly.

"Now hold on!" I protested. "This is no time for catechisms. I told you I'm a declines-to-state. An independent."

"Of what are you independent?" Hallowell asked.

"Of that Old Man in the sky with whiskers," I said.

Hallowell grinned. "Come on, Danbom," he said, "do you really think we believe in an old man in the sky, with whiskers?"

"I don't know," I said. "Maybe for you he shaved, but I'll bet he has a beard for Horowitz."

"Are you independent of your deepest feelings, Danbom?" Duff asked. "You say you love Ella. Are you independent of that?"

"What's Ella got to do with anything?" I asked.

"God is love," Duff said.

"Listen!" I cried. "There's a war going on!"

"Sure there is," Horowitz said, "you're right in the middle of it. You're the battlefield, Danbom."

I flopped down in the mud utterly whipped. "You guys sure picked a fine time," I said. "You sure picked a fine time to come at me with religion."

"We didn't pick it, Danbom," they said.

"Wait!" I cried. "Don't start talking at me in chorus! I'll take you on one at a time, but not three at once."

"You're not taking us on," Horowitz said. "We don't believe in an old man with whiskers either. Never have."

"Mythological projection," Hallowell said. "Been dead for years."

"Then what in hell are we talking about?" I asked.

"God," they said.

I moaned. I wanted to perish, but their eyes were fastened on me as though they expected a declaration. "You guys are as fouled up as I am!" I said. "The way you talk, God is all things to all men."

"Something to all men," Hallowell said.

"Something is better than nothing," Horowitz said.

"All right, then," I said, "some sort of something. But that's as far as I'll go."

They looked at each other. They nodded.

"It's a start," Duff said. "Your ultimate concerns, and deepest feelings are real, Charlie, and they have their basis in that some sort of something."

The rain fell. I sat there in the mud with my shoes full of water, staring at the hounds of heaven who had finally brought me to ground. I was too benumbed to confute them. I couldn't have if I'd wanted to. I might as well have tried to cut a furrow on the ocean with a plow. "All right," I said again.

They smiled and I fully expected them to move in and administer the *coup de grâce.*

As a boy at Interdom I'd seen the side arms of dogma brandished so often that I'd developed a kind of fatalism. Spell it backward and dogma is Am God, and every preacher I'd ever known had been a quick-draw artist; he'd snatch his dogma out of its holster and pump an innocent kid full of credo faster than I could say Tinker Bell. But the chaplains just smiled.

"What are you so happy about?" I asked belligerently. "You don't take any prizes, you know, sitting there with your pants in the mud."

Their smiles broadened.

"Go on," I said, "which one of you is going to get me? You've been baying at my heels ever since you got here, but I'm still a declines-to-state."

"That's fine," they said.

Hallowell fished in his pocket and brought out his pitch pipe. He blew a watery note which carried away, blending with the water in the creek. "Let's have a little song," he said, "to cheer us up."

They commenced to sing, even Horowitz joined, and presently, to our infinite surprise, the chorus swelled.

Eleven

THE chaplains hadn't completed the second verse of "Down By the Riverside" when a muted baritone voice sang out of the darkness.

"Ahhhh."

Hallowell stopped singing and got to his knees, listening alertly. "That was Sergeant Jackson," he whispered and blew another note on his pitch pipe.

The voice came again, closer now. "I'm goin' to walk with the Prince of Peace . . ." it sang.

"Down by the Riverside," Hallowell answered.

"Down by the Riverside," a third voice sang.

"That's Gruber," Hallowell said. "Tenor, A Company. The first one is certainly Jackson." He blew his pipe again and before the note died away, Jackson splashed through the water and dropped in our midst.

"Keep blowing," he gasped, "they're homing on the pitch pipe, Padre."

Hallowell blew a series of notes and got an answer each time and in the next ten minutes the sorriest-looking lot of choristers imaginable crawled out of the dark and grouped around us. They were the very picture of defeat.

When it seemed that the last man had answered the call, Jackson surveyed the group and asked them to count off. The choristers counted around the circle. Their total was twenty-three.

"Half a platoon," Jackson said, "and three officers," he added, nodding to the chaplains.

"We're dead," Horowitz said. "Have been for hours."

"Don't mind that," Jackson said.

"It concerns me," Horowitz said. "Being dead is a hard line to hew."

"A hard row to hoe," Hallowell said.

"How'd it happen?" Jackson asked.

"The colonel killed us," Duff said.

Jackson nodded solemnly. "That's a lousy deal," he said. "He shouldn't have done that."

"It's a goddamned atrocity," a Virgin tenor said.

The men, squatting in the mud, mumbled their assent. It was an atrocity, the kind of thing they'd read about in the newspapers. They looked at the chaplains and shook their heads woefully. "Those Escondido bastards ain't human," one man said.

Jackson sighed and stood up. "We're the only organized force A Company has left," he said. "We were about to surprise the Escondidos when some damned fool alerted a sentry and they dropped on us with everything they had."

"That must have been us," Hallowell said. "A sentry challenged us just before the fight started. Sorry, Jackson."

"How come they challenge you if you're dead?" a Virgin baritone asked. "Just like those dirty Escondidos to kill you first and challenge afterwards. If that's the way they're going to fight, to hell with them. It's not fair."

The men agreed and began grumbling among themselves.

"It appears we've fouled you up pretty badly," Duff said. "But we have this party waiting."

"Party?" Jackson wailed. "What is it, a freaking costume ball?"

"I mean a person, not a party."

"Who shall remain nameless," Hallowell hastened to add.

"You four dead men on your way to meet a nameless person and you blow the whole exercise. That's great," Jackson said. "Just great!"

"It wasn't their fault particularly," I said. "They were trying to help me."

"You're beyond help, Danbom," Jackson said. "We infiltrated, crept, crawled and guerrillaed right up to their outposts and were ready to spring when they chopped us. Captain Crowell is falling back to regroup, but the company is scattered all over creation. I don't think he has a chance unless somebody takes the pressure off." Jackson looked glum and hopeless, but then his face brightened and he looked up the hill. "The Escondido Command Post is up there," he said. "If we could make a diversionary attack it might give the captain the time he needs to reorganize."

"A suicide attack," Horowitz said.

"In your condition, Padre," Jackson said, "that shouldn't make any difference."

"I guess not," Horowitz said.

"How many Escondidos do you guess are up there, Jackson?" I asked.

"Hard to tell. Sixty or seventy. Depends how many they sent after us. It'll be two or three to one"

"Three to one has a nice ring to it," Duff said.

While listening to Jackson, the men had pulled their heads down between their shoulders like wet and miserable turtles. The letter V on their helmet liners gleamed softly and their ponchos glistened as the rain washed the mud away. "Come on, men," Jackson said, "let's show a little fat and happy Virgin spirit. Are we going to let those Escondidos walk all over us?"

The turtles pulled their heads deeper into their ponchos. They weren't responsive. They were wet, cold, defeated and forlorn.

"Come on, Marines," Jackson declared, "let's show a little of the old Gung Ho spirit! Your buddies are depending on you."

"Wish I was dead," one turtle mumbled.

"If there were any corpsmen or umpires around I'd shoot myself," another said.

Jackson turned to the chaplains. "You guys are the morale builders," he said. "Start building."

Horowitz turned to me. "We got to go over that hill anyway, right?" he said.

I nodded. "To get to Oceanside, we do."

Horowitz pushed himself up and cleared his throat.

"Men," he said, "the Escondidos put their pants on one leg at a time, just like the rest of us." He paused, frowning thoughtfully. "However, I did once know a man who put his pants on two legs at a time, and also a one-legged man who put only one leg in his pants. But it's not how you put your pants on that's going to win this engagement, if such it can be called."

"Hold on, Horowitz," Duff said, "let's not depend so much on the appeal to reason. Extraordinary conditions call for extraordinary measures."

Duff stood up and raised one hand heavenward. "Men," he declaimed, " 'the Lord at thy right hand shall strike through kings in the days of His wrath! Behold the whirlwind of the Lord goeth forth with fury, a continuing whirlwind; it shall fall with pain upon the head of the wicked.' "

Stirred by these ringing phrases, some of the Virgin turtles looked up.

Chaplain Hallowell rose and joined Duff. " 'Do I not hate them, O Lord, that hate Thee?' " he declared. " 'I hate them with an unfeigned hatred as they were mine utter enemies.' "

"That's a little strong, isn't it, Hallowell?" Horowitz asked. "The Escondidos are human, just like us."

"No they aren't," one of the turtles said.

"Love thine enemy," Horowitz said.

"Hogwash!" another turtle replied. "Those damned Escondidos are the cruddiest bunch of smart-ass goof balls that ever lived."

Jackson smiled. "All right, men, if that's the way we feel about it, let's go get 'em."

"Yeah," a couple of Virgins said belligerently.

The men stirred. They poked their faces out of their ponchos and looked up the hill. The Biblical oratory had revived their fighting mood. "We'll kill 'em for real," one Virgin said.

Jackson turned to Hallowell. "How about you taking command?"

Hallowell was startled. "Why me?" he asked.

"You've got the pitch pipe," Jackson said.

Hallowell glanced at the pitch pipe in his hand, then nodded. He was rather pleased. "All right, Sergeant," he said and he turned to the turtles. "Come on now, men, let's get organized. Bass section on the left; tenors on the right."

One Virgin was reluctant. "Tenor section," he grumbled. "Bass section, baritone section. Up there on the hill they got a weapons section, a mortar section, a bazooka section—"

"Come on, man," Hallowell said sternly, "where's your esprit de chorus! We're going to slaughter them with song!"

"Song shmong," the Virgin replied dully.

"You there," Horowitz growled, "fall in with the goyim and 'Sing unto God, ye kingdoms of the earth; O sing praises unto the Lord!' That's David, boy."

"Yes, sir," the reluctant Virgin replied smartly and he took his place with the tenors.

With both hands Hallowell signaled the men to rise. The Virgins rose as a body and grouped themselves according to their voices. Hallowell blew a note. "Mmmmm," he hummed.

"Mmmmm," the chorus responded.

"When we attack," Hallowell said, "we will sing 'Turn Back, O Man.' Give it all the volume you've got and they won't know what hit them. I'll signal with the pitch pipe. Mind your phrasing and come in right on the beat with a good firm tone. Any questions?"

There were no questions. The men coughed, snorted and spat, clearing their vocal cords for action.

Horowitz fumbled in his pack and brought out a shofar. "Excuse me, Field Marshal," he said with exaggerated deference, "but I doubt we'll all be able to hear that pitch pipe in the rain. I'll give a blast on the shofar."

"I'd prefer the pipe on this occasion," Hallowell said frostily. "That horn is liable to throw the men off pitch."

Horowitz' face darkened and he brandished the shofar under Hallowell's nose.

"It was good enough for Joshua and it'll be good enough for you," he declared. " 'And it shall come to pass, that when they make a long blast with the ram's horn, and when ye hear the sound of the trumpet, all the people shall shout with a great shout and the wall of the city shall fall down flat!' "

"Is there a wall?" Duff asked Jackson anxiously.

"Jericho, you *nahr!*" Horowitz cried. "Jericho. 'And Joshua did unto them as the Lord bade him; he houghed their horses and burnt their chariots with fire!' "

"He what their horses?" Hallowell inquired politely.

"Houghed, houghed!" Horowitz declared.

"I think it means to hamstring," Duff said.

"Hamstring!" Horowitz cried. "Houghed is houghed and there's no ham in it. He cut the horses down!"

"Hold on," Jackson said, "we don't have time for Biblical interpretations. Let's go. I'll take the point," and he moved off, up the hill.

"Right," Horowitz declared, and waving his shofar he followed Sergeant Jackson into the darkness. "When I blast, you pipe," he said to Hallowell. "And when you pipe we attack."

Hallowell issued his final instructions to the troops.

"Enunciate," he said, "enunciate. And mind the entrances." Then we spread out and went to meet the enemy.

We climbed silently up the mud-slick hillside, anchoring ourselves and helping the next man along. We gained the top and pushed on stealthily, nerves taut, knees weak.

Then it happened. Then, as always, unexpectedly the enemy appeared.

An Escondido sentry heard our squishing feet and was about to challenge when Horowitz rose in front of him.

Like a mountain Horowitz rose up, like a whale from the deep he rose. Up he rose like the Lion of Judah.

One great hand was stretched to heaven; he brought the shofar to his lips and he houghed as Joshua had houghed the horses of the kings of the Hittites, the Perizzites and the Jebusites. He houghed a great hough which shot a stream of muddy water twenty feet in the air.

The poor Escondido turned and ran squawking toward his lines.

Horowitz houghed again and the blast of the shofar caught the Escondido in the stomach like a ripsaw and cut him down; it hamstrung and threw him rolling to the ground.

Such a blast, such a *tuml*, such an unearthly screech had never been heard. Everything stopped, as the sun that other day had stopped for Joshua. Escondidos were paralyzed in mid-stride. Those who tried to yell found their voices gone.

There was an unnatural silence as the shofar bellow died

away and then we heard Hallowell's pitch pipe. One clear note.

Instantly the Virgin chorus attacked, singing:

"Turn back, O man, forswear thy foolish ways
Old now is earth, and none may count her days . . ."

It was glorious! We were a thousand voices. We rang and volleyed! We thundered! Jackson's great voice shook the clouds in their passage. And I sang too! I'd found my voice. I could hear the notes, not just thick and thin, not just B flat, but all the notes. I sang with all my heart and lungs as I galloped across the field with the enemy in full flight before me.

"Still wilt not hear thine inner God proclaim,
Turn back, O man, forswear thy foolish ways."

Escondidos croaked. They hopped, flopped, leaped and squeaked.

A charge of Knights Hospitalers into an encampment of Saracens could not have been more crushing. The Escondido troops simply evacuated. They threw their weapons down and ran—some fell to their knees and covered their heads. A group of stunned umpires raised their hands and backed away declaring themselves neutrals.

My voice carried gloriously; my feet hardly touched the ground. I was transported. I was real and the song was real and I was fighting my way to Ella.

"For Ella, Ella, Ella!" I howled.

Escondidos fell whimpering, covering their ears, praying for deliverance.

Horowitz blew the shofar again and it sounded like all of Hannibal's elephants trumpeting. Hallowell piped and the chorus hit the second verse like Cossacks.

We raced for the C.P. tent in the center of the plateau, slammed through the door bristling with song—and there was Colonel Pollard.

He stared at us, his face mottled green with terror.

He backed across the tent, the swagger stick trembling in his hand. His jaw worked, chewing air. His eyes fell on the chaplains and though they were covered with mud he dimly recognized the outline of their features. They had come back from the dead.

The colonel's eyes lost even their palest hue and fastened hypnotically on his quivering swagger stick. He stared at it for a moment as though he had never seen it, then the sap seemed to drain out of him. "It's fa-fat," he said and he sailed the swagger stick through the door of the tent and fell into a chair. "I give up," he muttered. He bowed his head and closed his eyes. "I just give up."

It was a terrible thing.

Duff started forward to console the colonel, but I caught him.

An umpire began jotting notes on his clipboard. "Who's in command here?" he asked.

"I'm the conductor," Chaplain Hallowell said.

The umpire looked up sharply. "The what?" he asked.

"The conductor," Hallowell said again. "They have a nice tone, don't you think?"

The umpire blinked his eyes and frowned confusedly.

Colonel Pollard's head bobbed as though he had fallen asleep.

Sergeant Jackson stepped between the umpire and the chaplains. "I'll accept the surrender in Captain Crowell's behalf," he said. And with one hand behind his back he motioned us to get out.

We backed out the tent door, slipped through the crowd of dazed Escondidos and ran to the far side of the hill. As we started down, smashing through the wet brush, we could see traffic lights on U.S. 101. In my eyes they blurred into a continuous stream of light leading to Ella.

We reached the bottom of the hill and trotted over the rough ground. It was raining heavily again and frequently one or another of us would fall to our knees and stagger up, but at last we arrived at the fence bordering the highway and slid under it.

We were on free soil.

The traffic slashing by on the wet highway threw water in our faces, but it was a kind of baptism, washing our illusions away. I looked back through the fence into that sprawling government preserve, that Eden, cloud coo-coo, never-never-land, that huge actor's laboratory and I felt the terror of expulsion and the liberation of the apple.

The chaplains mopped their faces and looked around wonderingly as though they'd just come out of a drugged sleep. "We'd better find Brandy before she gives us up for dead," Hallowell said.

We were a mile above Horno Canyon, so we slogged down the shoulder of the road with the traffic sailing by at sixty miles an hour. We were two hours overdue and it began to look as though Miss Pollard had given us up.

Then Hallowell spotted the car. He ran toward it and pulled the door open. Miss Pollard screamed.

"Brandy, it's me!" Hallowell cried. "Chaplain Hallowell."

Miss Pollard recognized us by our number rather than our faces, which were covered by grease and mud. "Freddie, I hardly knew you," she said.

Horowitz smiled wryly. "That's fine," he said, "not only dead, but disfigured."

"We bring you news of fresh victories," Chaplain Duff said. "The Virgins have triumphed over the Escondidos."

Miss Pollard was delighted. "I just knew A Company would win!" she said. "I prayed it would. Father's been such a stinker all along."

As we got into the car Chaplain Duff winked at me. "There, you see, Danbom?" he said. "There is efficacy in prayer."

"Chaplain," I said, "the secret weapons in this operation were a shofar and a pitch pipe."

Twelve

ON THE way to Oceanside, I sat in the back seat wedged between Chaplains Duff and Horowitz. The packs were on the floor, running water from all the rain-soaked Bibles, Talmuds, missals and hymnbooks.

As Miss Pollard drove we dug out some less wet clothes and squirmed into them under our ponchos. I wiped the muck off my face with a wet sock and ran my fingers through my hair trying to make myself recognizable, if not presentable.

"Now, Charlie," Miss Pollard said, "when we get there I want you to be very considerate. Ella's been through a great deal."

"You didn't really tell her I was dead, did you?"

"Well, not exactly," Miss Pollard said. "I told her you were in extreme danger, that there had been a number of casualties and that when I heard anything definite I'd let her know."

"That's as good as out-and-out lying," I said.

"All's fair in love and war, Charles," Miss Pollard said. "And in this case we've got both situations going, so a little lie isn't such a terrible thing. Ella could have said good riddance, you know."

"I suppose so," I said.

"And after all, Danbom," Chaplain Hallowell said, "not so very long ago you *were* spiritually dead, so Miss Pollard isn't a liar in the strictest sense."

"That's right, Danbom," Duff said, "from a dead atheist you've come around to believing in some sort of something."

"Is she a Jewish girl?" Horowitz asked.

"Wait a minute!" I cried.

"Neither death, nor life shall be able to separate us from the love of God," Duff said.

"Stop!"

"Whosoever believeth in Me . . ." Hallowell began.

"One more word and I'll go Moslem!" I cried. "I swear it! Praise be to Allah, the Lord of Creation, the merciful, the compassionate. . . ."

They were silent.

"You guys are theological grave robbers," I said.

They apologized.

"One step at a time," I said. "Let me straighten out my treasures here on earth, if any."

Miss Pollard was convulsed.

"With my luck," I said, "any religion I choose is likely to be a barrier between Ella and me. Right now it's like Russian roulette."

"She should be like Ruth," Horowitz said. " 'Intreat me

not to leave thee, or to return from following after thee; for whither thou goest I will go; and where thou lodgest, I will lodge; thy people shall be my people, and thy God my God.' "

"Look," I said, "I took one girl out of the Bible and she practically ruined me. You can bet I'll never do that again. I can't get rid of her."

"I think maybe you can now, Charlie," Miss Pollard said. "With luck maybe you can. After all, you seem to have joined the ranks of the twice born, and that's pretty good for an orphan."

We came into Oceanside and drove slowly down the esplanade to the Admiral Motel where Miss Pollard parked the car in the drive; there was a light burning in the office.

"Well," Miss Pollard said, "this is it. Any suggestions?"

"You take the point, Brandy," Hallowell said. "We'll support you and hold Danbom in reserve."

"Very good," Miss Pollard said.

They left me in the car and went up the path to the office.

I waited, listening to the rain drum on the convertible roof, a steady melancholy sound. The raindrops on the car windows glistened in the motel light. Each one seemed to cling to the glass, trying desperately to preserve its identity on that slick, perpendicular surface, but then another drop would hit it and they'd run down the window together smashing more drops and leaving a trail behind them like a shooting star.

A terrible feeling of transience gripped me. The thin shield which held me together seemed to be in imminent danger of rupturing so that I'd run down out of myself into a puddle with the packs, Bibles and soggy clothes.

Ella would go to Orlando. She would go and I'd become a prancing, dancing, recruiting poster Marine, a neatly programmed cardboard hero with a lovely cardboard girl and when my enlistment expired I'd sign over and over like clockwork. Thus it was decreed by the Universal Military Training Act as Amended.

Who could fight it?

Then, almost without volition, my lips began to move, speaking quietly over the sound of the rain.

"I say there, Some Sort of Something," I said, "if You'll forgive the use of pronouns in my address, I don't mean them in a definitive sense, but we're short of words for You down here; I mean all over, up and down are bogus orientations too, I know, but that's how we think. Well then, if You'll forgive all these shortcomings I'd like to make a request. I know it sounds like hedging a bet, or buying insurance, since I haven't been a regular adherent, or maybe I have been—I don't know—but the point I'm trying to get over is that I'd sure like to be honest with Ella. I don't mean this to sound like a concession, or like I'm giving up my independence, but I'd sure like to get to a place, or into a condition, where I could really live. Know what I mean? I mean live real. There's so much phony crap around, You know, that it's hard to do. Most folks don't even want to.

"I know I did my bit to add to the general fund of sin with the Girl from Escondido and all, and I'm really sorry about it. I truly am. I think it was phony and I'd sure like to get clear of it. But You've got to understand—there I go with pronouns again—that most people down here make their living at it, at being phony, I mean, not that this excuses me. I didn't mean it to sound like that. I'm guilty as hell, but I mean the advertising and military men, of which I'm in the latter category, find it tough sometimes not to swallow their own hogwash. So anyway, if You could see a way to help out in this instance I'd be undyingly grateful."

I felt better. "Oh, there's one other thing," I said. "I'd sure like to keep this dialogue, if it can be thought of in that manner, a secret from the chaplains. So if there's anything to this community of spirit idea don't tip them off about me. Not that I don't appreciate them, understand, but if it comes to the point of me choosing a church I wouldn't want the other two to think I was antipathetic, see? As far as I'm concerned Confucius was a good sort too. So, for right now let's keep this between us."

The rain stopped.

It just stopped abruptly and I had the crazy idea this was a sign. I even looked around for a rainbow and it was dark outside. Then the car door was jerked open and Chief Budd jumped in.

He was no answer to a prayer.

"Danbom!"

"Don't hit me!"

"Danbom, you sneaky bastard."

"I'm not sneaky."

"You son of a bitch."

"I refute that!"

"When they said you were dead I damn near died!"

He was beating me on the shoulder and to my astonishment he was grinning. "What's wrong with you?" I asked.

"Danbom, you have no idea what I've been through these last few hours. Ella almost drank the Mercurochrome. She threw a Juliet fit. Swore she'd never speak to me again. She loves you, boy. That's how crazy she is!"

"I love her," I said.

"Why in Christ's name didn't you say so?"

"I said so in my name," I said.

"Not to me, you didn't."

"I don't love you," I said.

"But goddamn it, I'm her legal guardian! You want to court Ella you have to ask my permission."

"That went out with union suits," I said. "You wouldn't have given it to me anyway."

"You think I'm nuts?"

"There you are."

Chief Budd's expression sobered. He grew canny. "Conditions change, Danbom," he said loftily. "Yes, they change."

"They seem to have," I said. "Where's Ella?"

"Inside, waiting for us to conclude our legitimate and necessary business."

"What business?"

"Well, Charlie," Budd said, "as you may know I've been transferred."

"Yes, I know."

"I've had a couple of bids on the motel here, but in a little town the word gets around when a man's over a barrel. The real estate sharks are out to rob me. I don't want to sell, but if I put a manager on the place, who knows what'll happen?"

"You'd probably have to pay him a salary," I said.

The chief scowled. "Don't bargain until you hear the deal," he said. "You don't hold all the cards."

"When are you leaving?"

"Day after tomorrow. Now here's the deal. If you promise to give up that broad in Escondido, and never see her again as long as you live, I'll give my permission for you to court Ella, providing you get her to manage the motel until I get back."

"What does Ella get?"

"Free rent."

"Some dowry."

Budd scowled. "Take it or leave it," he said.

"Chief, would you believe me if I told you I never had a girl in Escondido, or anywhere else?"

"No," he said.

"Well, it's true."

"Ella won't believe it either and if you start off lying to her I'm going to lose this motel and also I'm going to break your thick skull. All I want is your promise."

"I can't do it, Chief, because I'd be lying, but before you start swinging let me talk to Ella."

"You crud!" Budd cried. "You mean you won't give up that lousy tart for Ella?"

"Chief," I said, "I'll put the Girl from Escondido in your seabag when you leave. She'll be a comfort to you on Okinawa. And I'll throw in Whistler's Mother."

I pushed out of the car and the chief followed me up the path, trying to decide if he was going to let me reach the door alive.

I noticed the names on the cabins had been changed. Chief Budd, bellicose Budd, up and at 'em Budd with a hammer in his hand, had gone pacifist. The *Admiral Sherman* cabin was now the *George Fox.* There was an *Emerson* cabin, a *Gandhi* cabin; there was even a *Martin Luther King* cabin.

"What happened here?" I asked.

The chief frowned self-consciously. "Conditions change," he said. "Okinawa for the Okinawans, I say."

When we came into the living room the chaplains, Miss Pollard and Ella were gathered around the table. Ella was pouring coffee and there was a loganberry pie.

She looked at me and smiled tentatively. "Hello, Charlie," she said.

"Hello, Ella."

"I'm glad you're not really dead, or hurt, or anything."

"So am I," I said, but she seemed to be far away.

"I'm glad you came," she said.

"I had to," I said.

"Well, I'm glad."

She handed cups of coffee to the chaplains and Miss Pollard, then she poured one for me. "You must be cold," she said.

"I am," I said, "but that'll change in a second, or it'll go on forever. Coffee won't change it, or whiskey, or fire, or sunshine. Nothing can change it but you."

"I will if I can, Charlie," she said, and her not being sure she could change it scared me. It scared me more than being motherless and fatherless, more than being killed by the colonel, more than being shot at, exposed and despised, more than anything I could remember; because if Ella couldn't reach out and take my hand I knew I'd orbit in space like a lost astronaut until I died.

I was tempted to lie to her, strongly tempted to accept Miss Pollard's advice and go on pretending that I had a girl in Escondido to give up—but I couldn't. Ella's eyes rested on me, clear and questioning. She was waiting.

"Ella," I said, "I don't have anything I can give up for you. There's no sacrifice I can make. That's how poor I am."

"You don't have to make any sacrifice, Charlie," she said.

"I love you," I said.

She looked down at the coffee she'd poured for me. "Thank you, Charlie," she said.

"I thought I'd let you know."

"I guess I do."

I drew a deep breath and let it out slowly. "And Ella, there is no Girl from Escondido. There never has been."

Ella put the coffee cup down on the table and crossed the room to me. She cocked her head and looked into my eyes. "Charlie," she asked, "couldn't I be her?"

"Who?" I whispered hollowly.

"The girl you made up and dreamed about. Couldn't I be her some of the time?"

Her question took me by surprise. I couldn't think what to say.

"Couldn't I be, Charlie?" she asked again.

"Ella, she isn't real!" I protested.

"But Charlie," Ella said, "can't I be unreal sometimes too?"

"I don't know," I said. "I don't!"

"I'd like to be unreal for you, Charlie," she said. "Reality is awfully dull. Couldn't I be?"

"Well sure," I said. "I guess you could."

Ella lifted the Virgin helmet from my head. She stood on her toes and kissed me. "'His mouth is most sweet,'" she said, "'yes, he is altogether lovely. This is my beloved, and this is my friend, O daughters of Jerusalem.'"

And suddenly there was a rainbow in the room and we ran together like raindrops.

THE rain had passed and it was dark.

In the sky beyond Herzog's bulky outline I could see the Southern Cross resting on his right shoulder like an ornament. Down the tent row, men were talking and the air was sweet with the mustiness of jungle growth and decay.

Herzog's carbine lay loose and forgotten in his big hands. Presently he stirred and looked up at me. "Well, go on," he said.

"Go on what?" I asked.

"Finish," he said. "What happened to the colonel?"

"The umpires killed him," I said.

"Now that is fat!" Herzog said explosively. "That is really fat!"

"Exactly what the colonel said."

Herzog put his carbine aside. He stood up and began pacing the floor, his face pinched with the injustice of it. "Those chaplains were dead," he said. "They had no right to lead an attack. The colonel killed them."

"Retribution," I said. "The mills of the gods grind exceedingly fine."

"Oh, crap!"

"Also it was Easter Sunday," I said. "They had risen."

Herzog stopped and swung around, his eyes glittering with animal fury. "Danbom!"

"Okay. It wasn't Easter Sunday," I said.

"Danbom, I'm going to kill you!"

"How can you be sure?"

"I'll cut you in four pieces! They'll have to ship you home in tin cans."

"But my soul will go marching on," I said.

Herzog groaned and threw himself down on his cot. "God, I'll be glad when you're gone," he moaned. "You're the biggest liar that ever lived. The biggest!"

"You ought to read the newspapers," I said.

"I do."

"Well?"

"Well what!" Herzog demanded and he rolled over to look at me, his eyes clouded and sullen.

"According to them there's no war here, but we're winning it, right?"

"Winning nothing," Herzog grumbled.

"Maybe if we flew Disneyland over here we could win. Make them swap their rifles for a book of tickets."

"That is fat."

I shrugged. "Well, it's a program. Give the people what they need, like the newspapers."

"What happened to those other guys?" Herzog asked.

"They're still in the Corps as far as I know. Laperuta made Sergeant. I lost touch with Powell and Morgan. The last I heard about Weller was that the psychiatrists had straightened him out. For a time there it looked like it was going to take a frontal lobotomy."

Herzog studied the floor for a time, tracing a pattern on it with his finger, his chin resting on one forearm. "Did you get married?" he asked presently.

"I thought you said I was a liar."

"Sure you are!" Herzog bellowed. "But I want to hear the end of it anyway! You wasted all this time. I got a right to hear the rest. You said you knew an operation more fouled up than this one and you lied about that too!"

"We got married," I said. "Hallowell, Horowitz and Duff performed the ceremony."

"All three?"

"It was a mixed marriage. Holy wedlock with three locksmiths."

Herzog flipped over on his back and groaned.

"Miss Pollard and Captain Crowell got married at the same time."

"Yeah? I had a hunch she was going to go for Hallowell."

"She did, later."

Herzog sat up, scowling and furious. "What's that mean?"

"Well, Crowell got killed and Miss Pollard, his widow, married Chaplain Hallowell, later."

"Now that *is* a lie! That is a damned lie. You haven't been out here long enough for someone you knew in Pendleton to get killed and his wife marry a chaplain. That wouldn't even be decent!"

"I'm just trying to give you a happy ending," I said.

"Some happy ending! I want the truth."

"Do you really? Are you sure you can live with it?"

Herzog studied me suspiciously, warily. Then he nodded.

"Well," I said, "there was a First Battalion, 16th Marines at Pendleton. Colonel Pollard was the C.O. and I was in it. There were reserve chaplains on the base."

"Yeah," Herzog said, cautiously.

"We held a field problem."

"Yeah, go on."

"Because I'm an orphan they made me the chaplains' assistant."

"Because you're a goof-up they made you chaplains' assistant," Herzog declared.

"All right. Have it your way. But I did meet a girl."

Herzog nodded. "That's possible. What happened to the chaplains?"

"After their six weeks were up they went home. Hallowell went to Detroit; he's choir director in a big church there. Horowitz went back to his wife and kids in Jersey. Duff returned to his parish in Oakland."

"All right," Herzog said.

"You like that, do you?"

"Just give me the facts!" Herzog bellowed. "Never mind what I like!"

"The rest is just about like I said."

"And Miss Pollard married Captain Crowell," Herzog said.

"That's right. And Colonel Pollard is out here in the Military Assistance Command."

"I knew we had a bunch of dead heads topside," Herzog said. "How come you never showed me a picture of your wife?"

"You never asked me."

"All right, let me see one."

"As a matter of fact I don't have any."

"Danbom!"

I shrugged. "I simply don't, Herzog. I carry a picture of her in my mind."

"You lying creep! I missed chow to listen to all this guff. Show me a picture or I'm going to wring your neck."

"How can I if I don't have one?"

Herzog leaped up and crossed the tent. He shoved his hand in my face. "Give me your wallet," he demanded.

I gave him my wallet and he flipped through the pictures. "Why, you ain't even an orphan," he declared. "Who's this?"

"Whistler's Mother," I said. "A remembrance."

Herzog socked the wallet into my midriff and went back to his cot. "Oh, mother. Oh, Christ! It's going to be heaven when you leave tomorrow. Just plain heaven."

"I'm glad I can do that much for you," I said.

"Yeah, I'll bet you are," Herzog said truculently.

For a long time he sat hunched on his cot, studying his interwoven hands. When he finally spoke it was hardly a whisper. "Tell me about her anyway," he said.

I smiled. I lay back with my hands behind my head and began to recite: " 'My beloved spake, and said unto me, Rise up, my love, my fair one, and come away. For lo, the winter is past, the rain is over and gone; the flowers appear on the earth; the time of the singing of birds is come and the voice of the turtle is heard in our land."

Herzog listened enrapt and I spoke on into the dusky night: " 'My dove, my undefiled is but one; she is the only one of her mother, she is the choice one of her that bore her. The daughters saw her and blessed her; yea, the queens and the concubines, and they praised her. Who is she that looketh forth as the morning, fair as the moon, clear as the sun, and terrible as an army with banners?' "

When next I looked at Herzog he was smiling. He was rocking back and forth, half asleep, but because I'd stopped he glanced up. His eyes were warm, hopeful and friendly. "Who is she?" he asked.

"Ella," I said.

"Really?"

"I wouldn't lie about her, Herzog," I said.

He nodded. "Danbom, when I get out of this phony war can I come visit you?" he asked.

"Sure," I said. "I'll give you a card. Come to Oceanside." I took a card from my wallet and flipped it across the tent to Herzog.

He picked it up and read the name. "Song of Solomon Motel?" he asked.

"Yeah, we changed the name. It's gotten to be a very popular place."

Herzog studied the card, turning it over in his hand. "This the right phone number?" he asked.

"Sure," I said.

"Right address?" he asked.

"It's between Ecclesiastes and Isaiah," I said.

Herzog looked up sharply, then he snorted and tucked the card into his pocket. "Danbom," he said, "the truth is I'm going to miss you like hell when you're gone."

"Herzog," I said, "if and when I'm gone I'll miss you too."

"She'll meet you at the plane, I guess."

"Oh, sure," I said, "she'll meet me at the plane."

"Good," Herzog said. "Good, good."

"Good night, Herzog," I said.

"Good night, you lousy boondoggling creep," he said.

And we pulled our blankets around us to sleep.